WARNING:
This journal contains
wacky humor,
thrilling action,
nail-biting suspense,
a cool rap,
and a mind-blowing cliffhanger!

the misadventures of MAX CRUMBLY

MASTERS OF MISCHIEF

Also by
RACHEL RENÉE RUSSELL

the misadventures of MAX CRUMBLY

MASTERS OF MISCHIEF

BOOK THREE

RACHEL RENÉE RUSSELL

with Nikki Russell

ALADDIN

NEW YORK LONDON TORONTO SYDNEY NEW DELHI

ALADDIN • An imprint of Simon & Schuster Children's Publishing Division 1230 Avenue of the Americas, New York, NY 10020 • First Aladdin hardcover edition June 2019 • Copyright © 2019 by Rachel Renée Russell • All rights reserved, including the right of reproduction in whole or in part in any form. • ALADDIN and related logo are registered trademarks of Simon & Schuster, Inc. • For information about special discounts for bulk purchases, please contact Simon & Schuster Special Sales at 1-866-506-1949 or business@simonandschuster.com. • The Simon & Schuster Speakers Bureau can bring authors to your live event. For more information or to book an event contact the Simon & Schuster Speakers Bureau at 1-866-248-3049 or visit our website at www.simonspeakers.com. • Book designed by Karin Paprocki • The text of this book was set in Italo Medium Extended. • Manufactured in the United States of America 0419 FFG • 10 9 8 7 6 5 4 3 2 1 • Full CIP data for this book is available from the Library of Congress. • ISBN 978-1-5344-5349-4 (hc) • ISBN 978-1-5344-5350-0 (eBook)

To Arron Turner,
a Spider-Man fanatic since the day you were born,
a voracious reader, book reviewer,
and comic book collector,
and a super-talented YouTube creator.
YOU are a REAL hero!
Stay SMART, COURAGEOUS, and AWESOME!

THE MISADVENTURES OF MAX CRUMBLY
(IMPORTANT STUFF YOU NEED TO KNOW IN THE EVENT OF MY MYSTERIOUS DISAPPEARANCE)

1. TRAPPED IN THE DUMPSTER OF DOOM!

I knew middle school was going to be really hard, but I never expected to be BURIED ALIVE in a DUMPSTER full of ROTTING GARBAGE, wearing an ICE PRINCESS COSTUME and BIKER BOOTS!

Are we having FUN yet?! Give me a break!

My life as a wannabe superhero totally STINKS!

Okay, that FUNK-TASTIC stench I'm smelling is actually the Dumpster, not my life. But STILL . . . !

There's only ONE thing more HUMILIATING than being TRAPPED at my SCHOOL in a NASTY Dumpster in the middle of the NIGHT. And that's being trapped with ERIN MADISON, a ~~cute~~ computer whiz and the SMARTEST kid in the entire school. And . . . NO! I'm NOT crushing on her!

Any minute now we're going to get ARRESTED by the POLICE and thrown in JAIL for trespassing, destruction of property, and several FELONIES! . . .

FINALLY! Here is my chance to be a REAL SUPERHERO and ~~rescue Erin~~ get us out of this Dumpster before it's too late.

If this were a scene in my favorite superhero comic book, it would go down like this:

When we last left our courageous hero and his ~~CRUSH~~ trusty sidekick, they were sitting in a pile of rotting mystery meat, smelly gym socks, a vomit-stained mattress from the cot in the school nurse's office, and other frightfully foul things, hopelessly TRAPPED within four inescapable brick walls as police officers raced to the scene.

Will our desperate dynamic duo be DOOMED by this dreadful and disgustingly dirty DISASTER?!

Or will they be FRUSTRATED by their feeble failures to flee this filthy fifteen-foot fortress?!

Can our heroes use their supersmarts and uncanny creativity to build two antigravity energy beams from the random recyclable junk in the Dumpster?!

Just keep reading to discover if our Masters of Mischief will escape this cataclysmic catastrophe and bravely BLAST OFF into the night sky like two blazing ROCKETS!...

ERIN AND ME, BLASTING OFF . . .

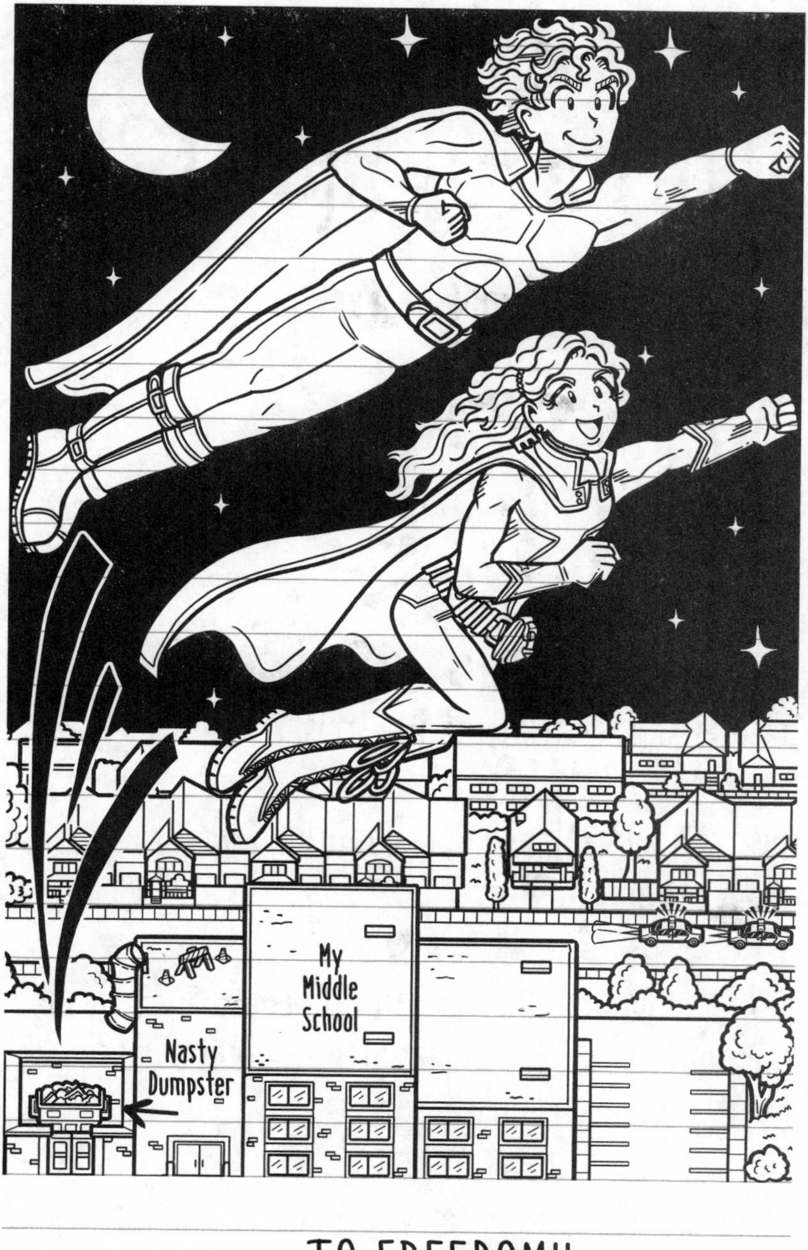
My Middle School
Nasty Dumpster

. . . TO FREEDOM!!

FREAKING AWESOME!! RIGHT?!

Hey! This could actually happen!

NOT!!

Superheroes make it look EASY to get out of an IMPOSSIBLE situation like this.

But let's be real, people. I don't have any superpowers!

Yet somehow I pulled off an EPIC capture of three criminal MASTERMINDS planning to steal our school's expensive new computers!

Okay, so maybe they weren't exactly masterminds.

"MEATHEADS" is probably a better description. Even though they had the combined IQ of a red crayon, they were mean, ruthless, and very dangerous!

Erin and I teamed up and declared WAR on them earlier tonight.

It was like a real-life video game battle, only ten times SCARIER! I'd had Erin's phone with me, and she'd been "playing" along from home on her computer, helping me set traps in the school. It took us hours, but we kicked their butts and took them out one at a time.

In the end, not only did we outsmart them, but we booby-trapped those three MENACES and then left them at school for the authorities to find.

Those guys will NEVER roam free again!!

Don't believe me?

Here's my PROOF! . . .

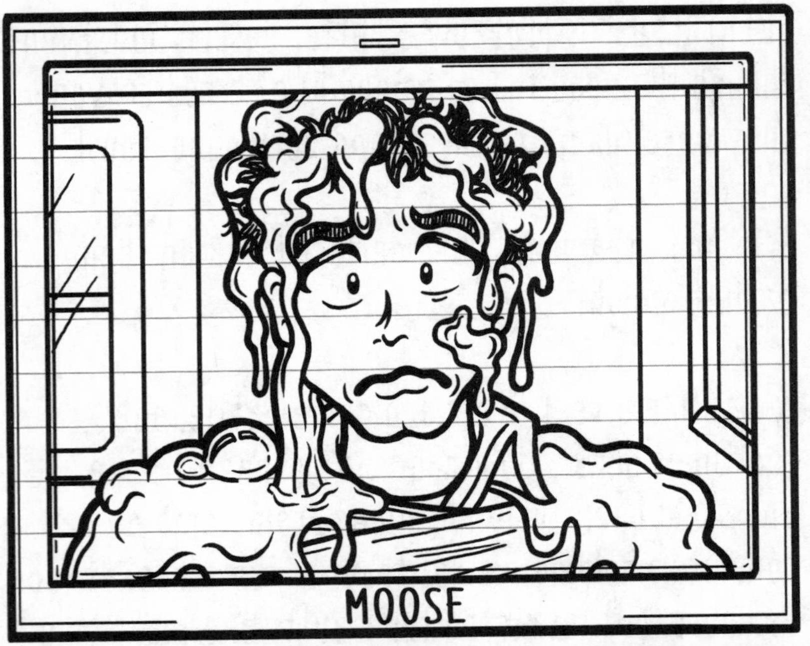
MOOSE

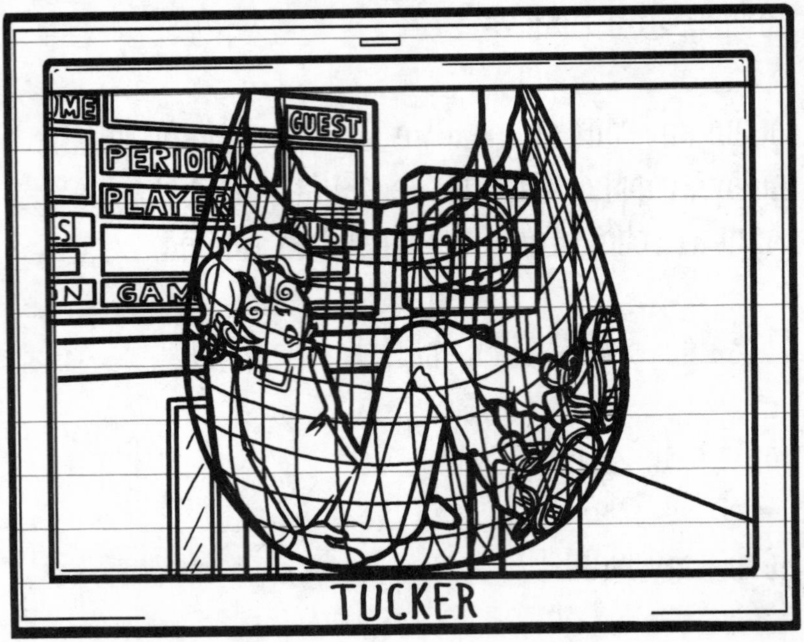
ME
GUEST
PERIOD
PLAYER
LS
ULS
ON
GAM
TUCKER

RALPH

The only problem is that unless Erin and I can figure out how to get out of this STUPID Dumpster, WE might never roam free again either!!

FOR REAL!!

It's all MY fault that she's in this HOT MESS!

Anyway, we don't hear the sirens anymore.

But that's because the POLICE have arrived and are parked right outside this brick wall!

We're both totally FREAKING OUT!

I'm not going to lie to you. Things are looking pretty BLEAK for us right now.

That's WHY I'm documenting everything in my journal: *The Misadventures of Max Crumbly*!

If the police actually find me, they'll probably throw me in the SLAMMER for:

1. unlawfully trespassing on school property

2. intent to do great bodily harm with deadly plastic cling wrap

3. assault and battery with a basketball hoop

4. cruel and unusual use of a python as a dangerous weapon

And, last but not least, the most serious and heinous offense . . .

5. vicious crimes against fashion (did I mention that I'm wearing an ice princess/superhero costume?!).

Hopefully, one day someone will find my journal hidden in this Dumpster.

Then the entire world will learn the truth about the night I MYSTERIOUSLY disappeared and NEVER returned to South Ridge Middle School!

Even if I'm not able to save MY life, I'll at least save ERIN'S.

And maybe even . . . **YOURS!**

Hey, I'm not trying to be all super DRAMATIC. But by the time you read this, I'll probably be ROTTING in PRISON and working on my NEW escape plan! . . .

ERIN, BRINGING ME A VERY YUMMY
SLEDGEHAMMER CHOCOLATE CAKE
WITH HACKSAW ICING!

But don't get it TWISTED!

I haven't given up . . . YET!

Sorry!

But Max C. is NOT going down like THIS!!!

WARNING!

This journal might end with a big, fat CLIFFHANGER, just like my first two!

So if you're going to have a meltdown, you should probably stop reading this NOW!

Maybe your parents will read you a cute bedtime story about a fuzzy baby bunny instead.

Otherwise, buckle up and get ready for yet another gut-wrenching roller-coaster ride through the halls and horrors of middle school.

Now let's say it all together, people....

BEEN THERE!

DONE THAT!

GOT THE T-SHIRT!!

Hey, no worries.

I GOT THIS!!

2. MIGHTY MOUTH STRIKES AGAIN

So, you're probably wondering how Erin and I ended up trapped in this stupid Dumpster.

I was on the roof and accidentally fell down a construction chute right into it. . . .

I busted Erin's cell phone when I landed in the Dumpster!

And when Erin couldn't get in touch with me, she snuck out of her house and came to the school.

She found me trapped in the Dumpster area and tried to rescue me by pulling me up over the wall.

Then SHE accidentally fell into the Dumpster too!

So there we were! Both stuck in a STINKIN' trash heap!!

The good news was that we finally came up with a brilliant plan.

We were going to hide out in the Dumpster (like we had a choice!) and try to escape AFTER the police found the three burglars inside the school, finished their investigation, and left.

But there was a very real DANGER that WE could end up BUSTED!

While searching the school for suspects, it was possible the police could find us hiding in the Dumpster and arrest US instead!...

ERIN AND ME, GETTING ARRESTED FOR . . . UNLAWFUL LOITERING . . . IN A DUMPSTER . . . AFTER MIDNIGHT?!

"I just wish we could SEE what was going on out there," I muttered in frustration.

I stood up and stared at the top of the wall, trying NOT to think about whatever just SQUISHED under my foot.

EWWW!!

Then I pulled my dad's comic book out of my boot to make sure it was okay.

Erin's eyes widened in surprise. "OMG! MAX, YOU ACTUALLY FOUND THE COMIC BOOK?!"

Yep, I'd finally managed to rescue my dad's SUPER-RARE, SUPER-VINTAGE, SUPER-VALUABLE comic book from those MANIAC criminals!

But I'm not gonna lie!

It took some serious guts and nerves of steel to get it back.

I was out on the roof, trying to grab the comic book after one of the burglars had maliciously tossed it out a window.

Looking back, it was a super-risky, super-stupid thing to do, because that was how I accidentally fell into the Dumpster. But after all the trouble I went to getting my hands on it again, there was NO WAY I was leaving without it!

"Yeah, I got it back." I shrugged. "No BIGGIE!"

Erin smirked and rolled her eyes at me.

Actually, it was a REALLY big deal! I'd crawled through miles of air vents on my hands and knees, gotten covered in toilet sludge, fought off three menacing criminals, befriended a ten-foot-long python, and almost FALLEN to my DEATH!

I just thought Erin should know I am an extremely BRAVE, SMART, ADVENTUROUS, SUPER-COOL DUDE! . . .

ME, TRYING REALLY HARD TO IMPRESS ERIN!

I carefully tucked the comic book back inside my boot for safekeeping.

Then I hoisted myself up onto the side of the Dumpster and balanced on a narrow ledge while I tried to reach the top of the wall.

"Max, please be careful!" Erin whispered. "If you fall, you could break an arm or leg, or worse! And if something happens, I'll just . . . !"

I turned and stared at her in surprise. She seemed to be genuinely worried about me.

Suddenly my palms started to sweat.

Erin actually CARED! SWEET!!

But my warm and fuzzy thoughts disintegrated into thin air when she nervously cleared her throat and continued. "I'll just have to throw my ice princess costume away if it's ripped or stained. I guess I can always make another one. Why ARE you wearing it, anyway?"

Well, THAT cleared up any confusion.

Erin only cared about her STUPID ice princess costume.

WHY are girls SO ding-dang obsessed with CLOTHING?!

I could fall off that wall and crack my cranium, splinter my spleen, bust my butt, and fracture my face trying to RESCUE her! And ALL she's worried about are the STAINS on her ice princess costume!!

So what am I? CHOPPED LIVER?!

Thank you for caring, Erin.

Anyway, standing on the edge of the Dumpster, I wasn't even close to seeing over that wall.

Don't get me wrong—I'm no munchkin! That wall was just ridiculously high!

WHY the heck does our school lock up our GARBAGE in a fortress with fifteen-foot-high brick walls and steel doors, while our brand-new computers, worth $100,000, sit in an unlocked room where anyone can easily STEAL them?!

GO FIGURE!. . .

HOW MY SCHOOL PROTECTS ITS WORTHLESS GARBAGE!! . . .

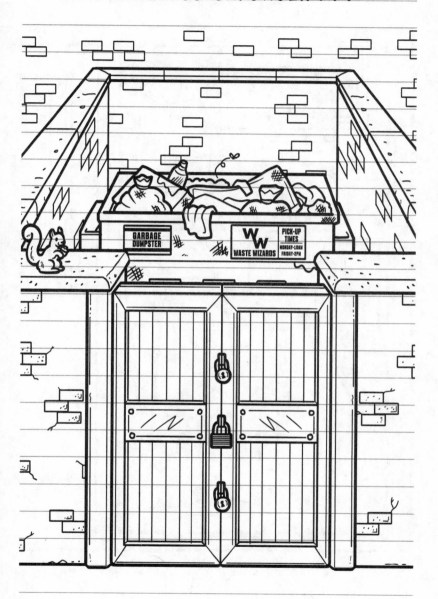

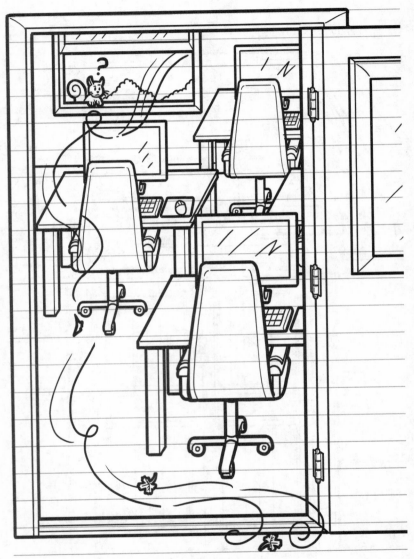

This made no sense WHATSOEVER!

"Listen, Max! Maybe the TWO of us will be tall enough to see over the wall!" Erin said.

She climbed up and balanced next to me on the edge. "You boost ME up, and then I'll pull YOU up. Okay?"

I was suddenly way too distracted to answer her.

My nostrils were filled with the most amazing scent.

It was a combination of cupcakes, Skittles, and Snuggle dryer sheets.

"MAX?!" Erin said, snapping her fingers in front of my face. "Earth to Max!"

I blinked. "Oh, sorry. I was just distracted by that . . . smell!"

"What smell?" she asked, glancing at the Dumpster.

"Actually, I think it was YOUR . . . smell!" I said awkwardly.

I have this habit of being brutally honest. My mom says it's always GOOD to tell the truth, but I'm not so sure.

I think she changed her mind after she asked me how her homemade zucchini bread tasted.

Sure, I may have used the words "soggy diaper" and "dirty toenails" to describe the taste. . . .

MOM

ME, TASTE-TESTING MOM'S ZUCCHINI BREAD

But I was being HONEST!

So I was totally confused when Mom got an attitude about the whole thing.

"REALLY, MAX?! Is THAT what you think my zucchini bread tastes like?! GET OUT OF MY KITCHEN! NOW!" she yelled at me.

I couldn't believe she actually did that.

The fancy gourmet chefs on those cooking shows on TV don't get kicked out of the kitchen when they tell a contestant their soup tastes like Cheerios and warm vomit.

I never even got a chance to tell Mom the chopped bits of zucchini in her bread looked and tasted exactly like boogers.

I was like, WHY ARE YOU TRIPPIN', MOM?!

DON'T ASK FOR MY OPINION AND THEN TURN INTO A HATER! WHAT'S UP WITH THAT?!

* 27 *

But it looked like Big Blabbermouth Max had struck again, because Erin looked totally offended. I guess my comment about her smell came out completely wrong.

"Whatever!" she muttered. "You don't smell so good right now either. Just boost me up, please!"

I was SO disgusted with MYSELF!

REALLY, MAX?! You finally have a chance to get this close to an AMAZING girl, and the first thing you do is insult her by telling her she STINKS?!

I KNOW! I totally messed up. I needed to do something to really impress her. Like maybe show her how STRONG I was?

Okay, I'll admit I'm not the muscular, athletic type.

But my ability to draw HUMONGOUS muscles on my mirror with toothpaste had drastically improved with practice....

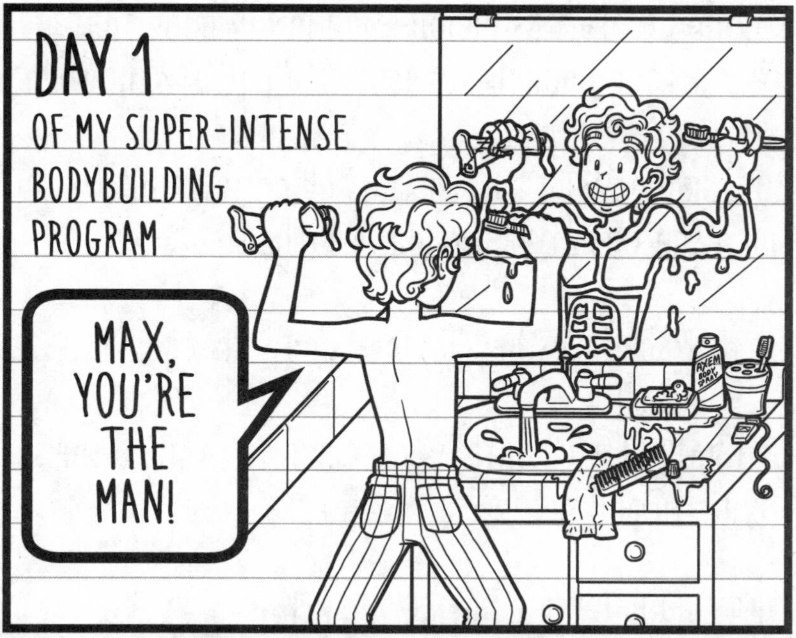
DAY 1
OF MY SUPER-INTENSE BODYBUILDING PROGRAM
MAX, YOU'RE THE MAN!
AXEM BODY SPRAY

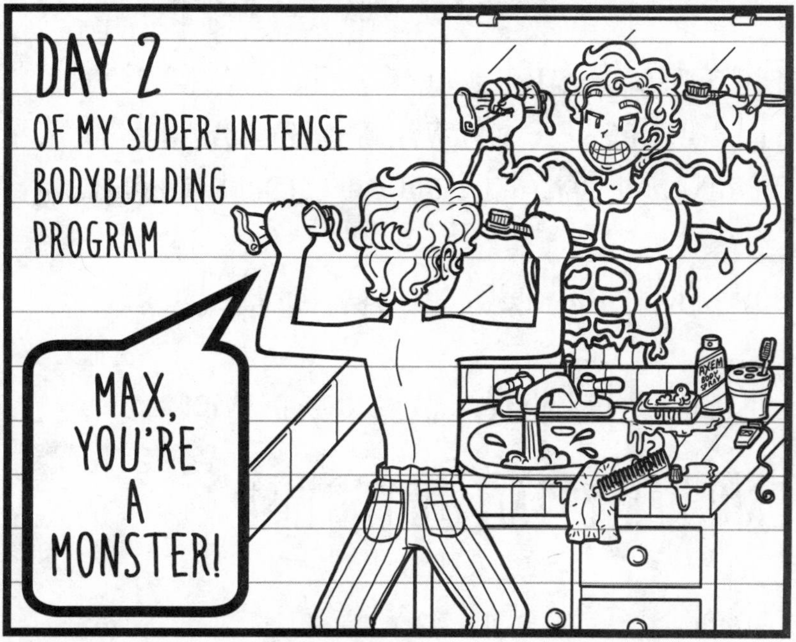
DAY 2
OF MY SUPER-INTENSE BODYBUILDING PROGRAM
MAX, YOU'RE A MONSTER!
AXEM BODY SPRAY

Anyway, there was no question in my mind that I was strong enough to boost Erin up onto the wall.

But I had no idea how she was going to pull ME up, when she wasn't able to do it earlier.

What if she loses her balance and falls again?

Or what if I accidentally yank her down while she's trying to pull me up?

We could be STUCK in this Dumpster FOREVER!

The authorities will probably find our skeletons STILL sitting here five years from now, which means we'll BOTH miss our high school graduation!

How CRAPPY will that be?!

I just need to CHILLAX and stop worrying.

ERIN HAS TOTALLY GOT THIS!!

I hope!

3. ERIN AND I FALL FOR EACH OTHER (KIND OF)

I looked through the Dumpster for anything that might help us escape.

How would the Incredible Hawk, superhero in my soon-to-be-bestselling comic book series, get out of here?

Well, that's easy. He would fly! DUH!

But unless I could figure out how to make myself some wings out of moldy textbooks and rotting tuna casserole leftovers from the cafeteria, I wasn't flying out of here anytime soon.

Then it hit me. . . . MY UTILITY BELT!!
(My belt didn't hit me. That would have hurt. The IDEA hit me!)

Not all superheroes have powers. Sometimes they just utilize quick thinking and cool gadgets. You know, like Bruce Wayne.

I was about to take off my belt!

"Um, Max?" Erin said, covering her eyes. "I don't think NOW is a good time for a costume change."

"No, look!" I pointed at a hook sticking out of the top of the wall, right next to where Erin was standing. "We could attach my belt to that hook and—"

"HANG ourselves in SHEER desperation!" Erin interrupted sarcastically.

"Of course NOT!" I answered. "I'm going to scale that wall like Batman does! It's going to be totally EPIC!"

That's when Erin burst into laughter so loud I was worried the cops might hear her.

"Max, you must have hit your head when you landed in the Dumpster. Dude, are you serious?!"

Okay, BAD idea! Instead, I hoisted Erin up on my shoulders and tried my best NOT to fall over. . . .

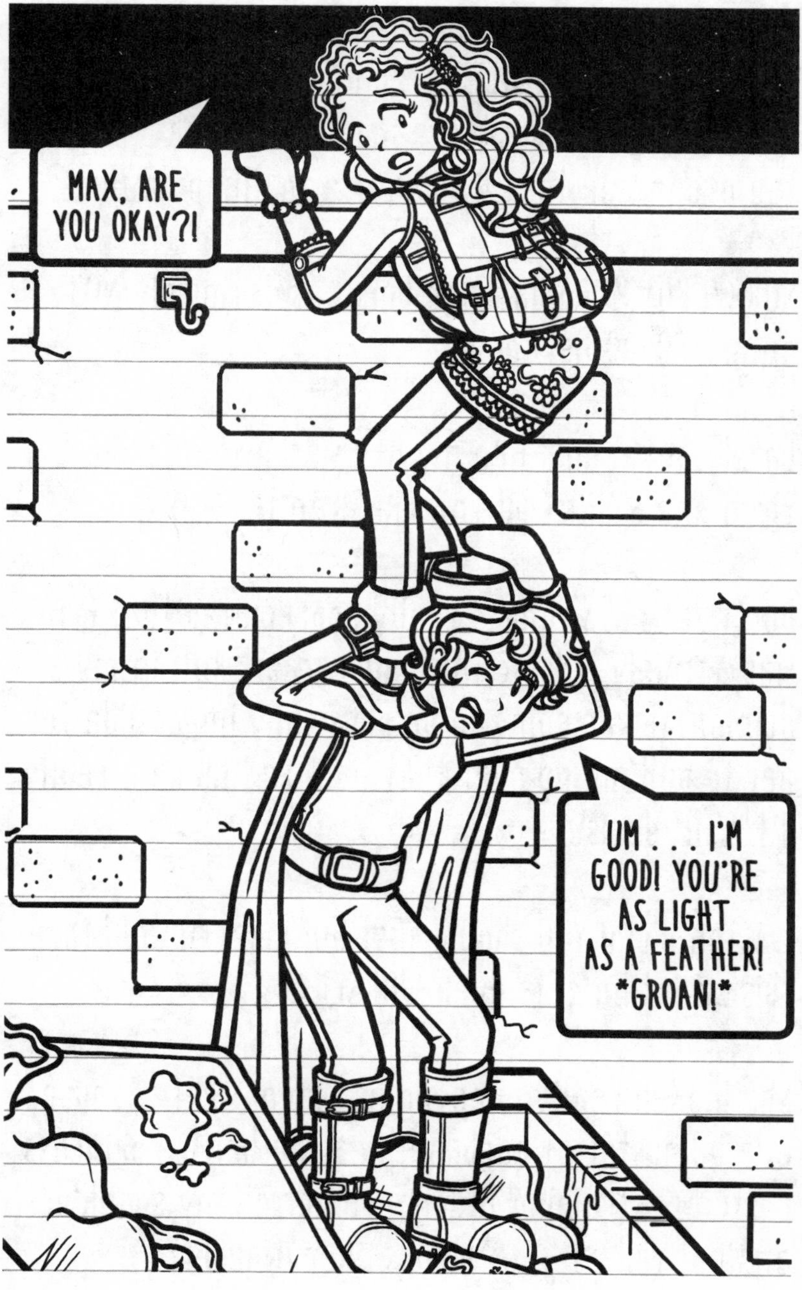
MAX, ARE YOU OKAY?!
UM . . . I'M GOOD! YOU'RE AS LIGHT AS A FEATHER! *GROAN!*

Erin cautiously peeked over the edge of the wall. "Good news!" she whispered down to me. "All the cops are inside. And there are some trash bins on the other side that we can use to climb down."

SORRY! But MORE garbage bins was definitely NOT on my TO-DO list tonight.

Lately, it seemed like my life was just jumping from one STINKY pile of TRASH to the next!

Don't get me wrong—I really appreciated that Erin was actively helping with our escape. But, in my opinion, it was going to be physically impossible for her to pull me up over that wall. So I made a really difficult decision.

"Listen, Erin! You should just GO! Right now! Before this situation gets even WORSE!"

She looked really annoyed as I stood there trapped in a Dumpster of garbage, wearing her ice princess costume, straining to balance her on my shoulders and not fall over, with cops everywhere!

Maybe it was a little difficult for her to imagine HOW this situation could actually get WORSE.

(There were valid reasons I was wearing an ice princess costume, but I don't have time to go into them right now. So just trust me. It seemed like a good idea at the time.)

"Don't be stupid, Max!" Erin sighed. "I'll just pull you up, and then we can leave. TOGETHER!"

Every minute she wasted helping me was a minute she was NOT escaping. I tried to reason with her. "Erin, I'm the whole reason you're in this MESS! Because of me, you hacked into the school's surveillance system, lied to your parents, and had your laptop confiscated! Then you snuck out of your house in the middle of the night to help ME, and now you're STUCK in a Dumpster surrounded by the police! You DO realize you're going to be grounded until your twenty-first birthday, right?!"

DANG! When I put it like that, I had no idea WHY she was still hanging around.

"Exactly!" Erin agreed. "Why would I abandon you now when we're SO close to getting out of here?"

She DID have a really good point! Take it from me, aspiring superheroes. Make sure you have a sidekick who's RIDE OR DIE!

And bonus points if she smells like cupcakes, Skittles, and Snuggle dryer sheets.

Right then I felt like Erin and I were INVINCIBLE! We could accomplish ANYTHING! But that wonderful feeling lasted only about thirty seconds.

"OMG!" Erin exclaimed. "The cops are coming back! Max, I need to hurry and pull you up so we can— WHOOOA!!"

Erin shrieked as she suddenly lost her balance and teetered back and forth and back and forth on my shoulders. Of course, that made me lose MY balance, and I teetered back and forth too.

Finally, we BOTH toppled over backward and . . .

. . . CRASH-LANDED IN THE DUMPSTER!

We just lay there, stunned, sprawled out on top of the garbage like discarded mannequins.

Luckily, we landed on that old mattress. Although we were pretty shaken up, we were really happy we didn't have any broken bones.

"Erin, what did you see out there?!" I asked.

Her eyes were HUGE with worry. "FOUR cops and a police DOG. WE NEED TO GET OUT OF HERE, MAX!! NOW!!"

Things quickly deteriorated from bad to worse. We heard the crackle of a police radio WAY too close for comfort. . . .

"Sarge, I just heard a noise from inside a brick storage enclosure out here. But it just might be rats. Do you want me to check it out?" he asked.

"RATS?!" Erin and I both gasped in horror.

It never occurred to us that there could be RATS in our Dumpster! But why not?

Rats from miles around would live in an all-you-can-eat buffet of cheap, nasty, rotten food.

NOT the Dumpster! The SCHOOL CAFETERIA!

And if there were RATS in the Dumpster, maybe there were also poisonous SPIDERS, venomous SNAKES, and soul-sucking DEMENTORS!

Hey, it could happen!!

"Got it! I'll investigate and secure the perimeter, Sarge," the officer responded.

That's when the dog started barking like crazy. I couldn't help but wonder how painful it would be to be torn apart by a RABID police dog!

But don't get it twisted! I LOVE dogs! I even volunteer at Fuzzy Friends Animal Rescue Center with my friend Brandon.

But THOSE dogs aren't trained to ATTACK on command!!

"What's that, Buster?" the officer said. "You think there's something inside? Let's go take a look!"

OH, CRUD! WE WERE SO DEAD!!

Erin and I just stared at each other frantically.

But if our eyeballs had vocal cords, they would have been SCREAMING hysterically.

We didn't have a choice but to dig into the DIRTY, STINKY, MOLDY, ROTTING pile of GARBAGE until we had completely buried ourselves from sight. Like some kind of WEIRD . . . HALF-HUMAN, HALF-MOLE . . . DUMPSTER-LOVING . . . FREAKS!

All while trying really hard NOT to think about the RATS!!

I HATE my life!!

FOR REAL!

4. HELP! DEADLY DUMPSTER ~~RATS~~ DOG!

If you think being buried alive in garbage or attacked by a vicious police dog was the WORST thing that could happen to us, I have some shocking news!

There was another threat ten times more dangerous.

WHAT was it?!

Being EATEN ALIVE by a dozen huge, dirty Dumpster RATS with fat, scaly tails, matted brown fur, dull, lifeless black eyes, and very sharp, pointy teeth.

Okay, Erin and I didn't actually SEE any of these deadly Dumpster rats.

But STILL!!

We had every reason to be really worried that at some point we WOULD.

And it was probably going to be HORRIBLE. . . .

ERIN AND ME, SURROUNDED BY DANGEROUS AND DEADLY DUMPSTER RATS!

Thank goodness we hadn't seen any Dumpster rats so far.

PRO TIP: When trying to hide in a ton of stinky garbage, do not breathe, because you will accidentally inhale or swallow something that's definitely NOT meant for human consumption.

For this reason, we decided to just hide BEHIND that old mattress instead.

First, the thick padding offered protection from violent attacks by dogs, rats, and dementors.

And second, after smelling the mattress up close, we were pretty sure one whiff of that STANK would KNOCK that police dog OUT COLD!!

We heard footsteps, and then the officer unlocked and slowly opened the huge steel door. . . .

SCREEEEEEEEECH!

We held our breath and peeked over the mattress. The officer stood at the entrance, talking into his radio while his dog nervously paced in circles, sniffing the ground and barking. . . .

AN OFFICER,
CHECKING OUT OUR DUMPSTER

We didn't dare make a sound!

"What is it, boy?!" the officer asked.

Just then the radio crackled again, and a garbled voice came through. "Hang on, Sarge!" the officer said. "I need to move outside this brick wall to hear you better. . . ."

Erin and I sighed in relief as the officer wandered away in search of better reception.

"Okay, Sarge, can you hear me now?! No?! Well, how about now?! Is THIS any better?! No?!" he asked as his voice grew fainter and fainter.

If only that officer had taken his PESKY dog with him, we could have escaped through that open door and made it HOME in less than fifteen minutes. Now I had to rely on my extensive experience and training with canines.

"What should we do?" Erin whispered, staring nervously at the barking dog.

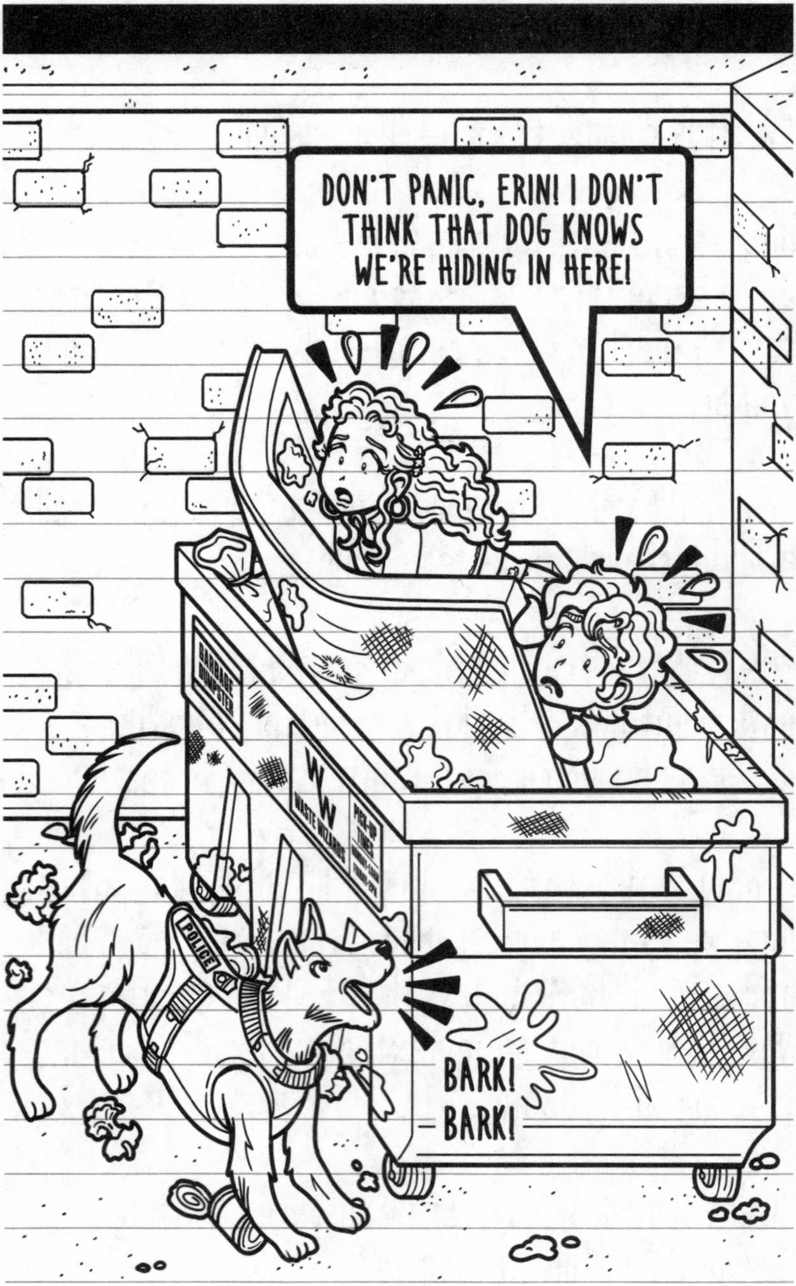
DON'T PANIC, ERIN! I DON'T THINK THAT DOG KNOWS WE'RE HIDING IN HERE!
GARBAGE DUMPSTER
WASTE WIZARDS
POLICE
BARK! BARK!

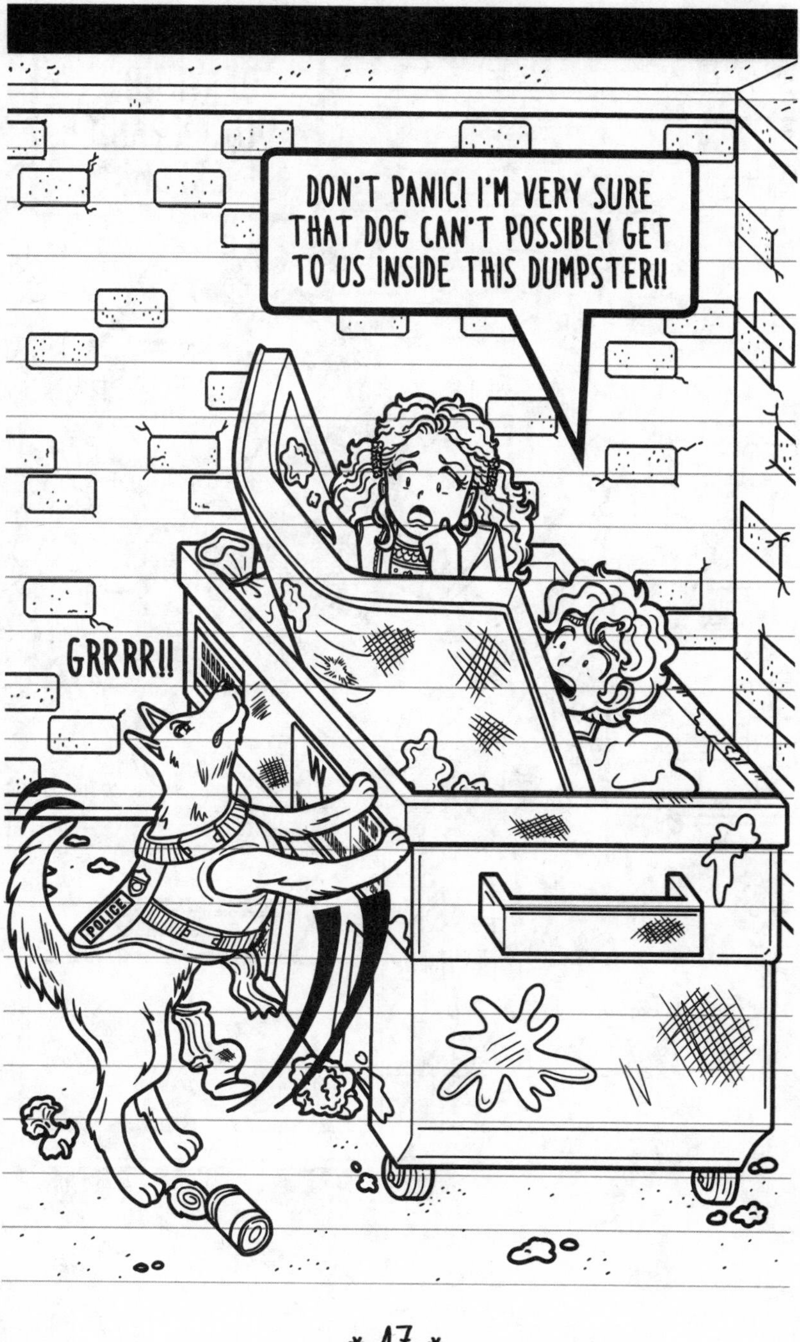
DON'T PANIC! I'M VERY SURE THAT DOG CAN'T POSSIBLY GET TO US INSIDE THIS DUMPSTER!!
GRRRR!!
POLICE

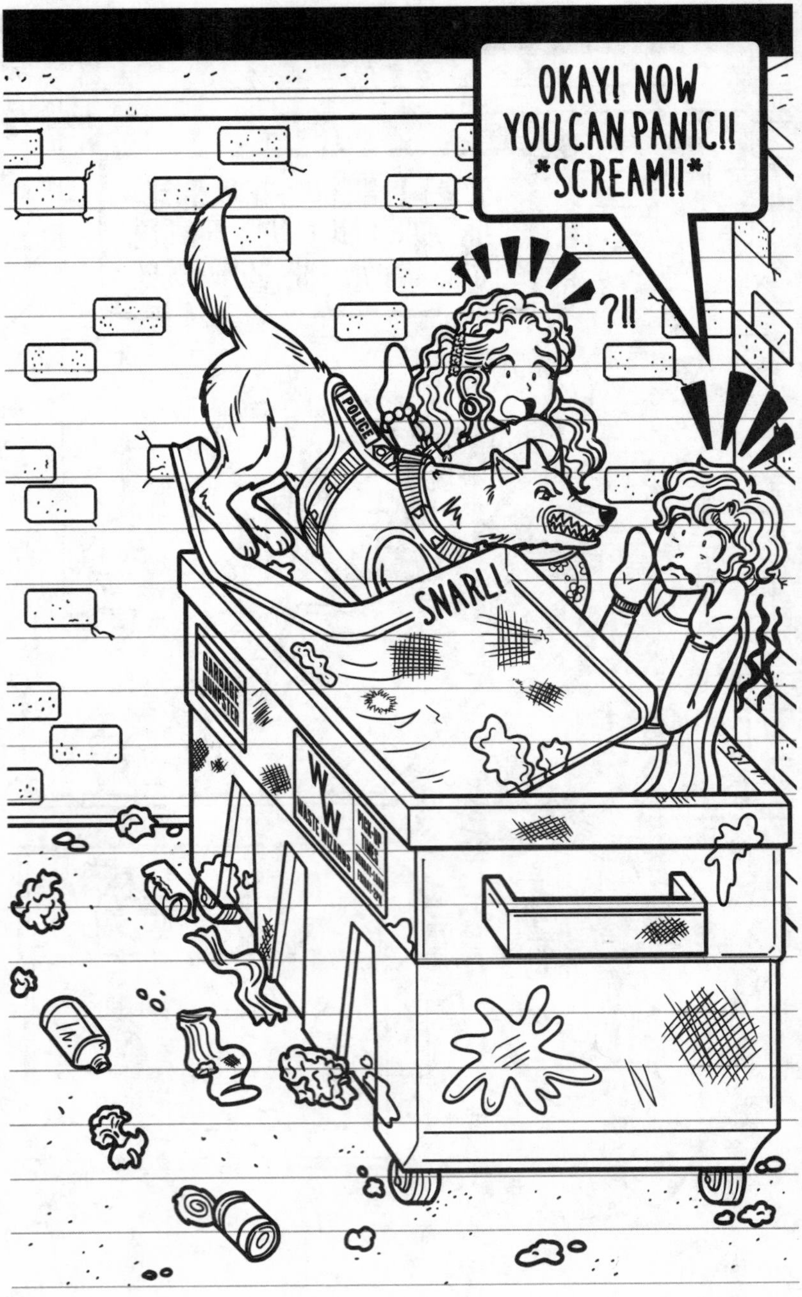
OKAY! NOW YOU CAN PANIC!! *SCREAM!!*
?!!
POLICE
SNARL!
GARBAGE DUMPSTER
WW
WASTE WIZARDS
PICK-UP TIMES

The dog snarled and bared its teeth. I suddenly felt as vulnerable as an extra-large Mighty Meat Monster pizza from Queasy Cheesy! The dog was about to ATTACK! Erin looked terrified. I HAD to do something!

"NICE DOGGIE!" I muttered, extending my hand to let him sniff it the way Brandon had taught me at Fuzzy Friends.

Of course, my hand was covered in Dumpster sludge. But dogs LOVE really stinky things! Right?!

The dog ignored my hand and instead lunged at my FACE, knocking me over onto my back! My heart was pounding in my chest. I knew I was DEAD MEAT!!

Until the dog gave me a BIG, WET, SLOPPY LICK!

"THUMPER?!" I cried as the dog happily wagged his tail nonstop and smothered me with doggie kisses. "Do you remember me, boy?! Sure you do!"

"THUMPER?!" Erin muttered, confused.

I pointed to the dog's back leg and then rubbed his belly. . . .

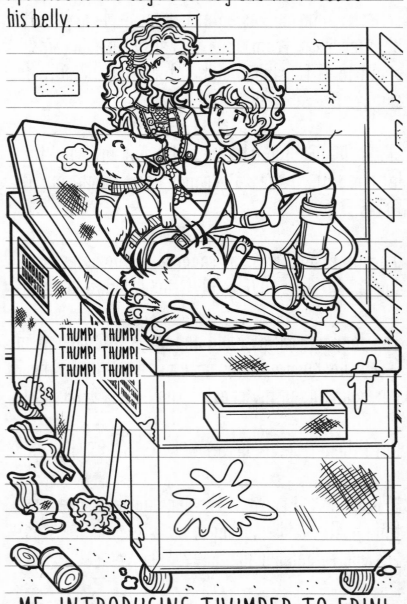

THUMP! THUMP!
THUMP! THUMP!
THUMP! THUMP!

ME, INTRODUCING THUMPER TO ERIN!

He happily thumped his back leg on a pile of super-rank cottage cheese, splattering it everywhere.

"Um . . . it seems like you know this dog?" Erin sputtered, wiping curds off her face. "Really well!"

"Thumper and I go way back!"

"I thought his name was Buster," Erin said.

Thumper flattened his ears, looking insulted.

"I guess that's what they call him now that he's a police dog! But Thumper used to be a rescue at Fuzzy Friends. He was so smart, the police canine unit picked him out and trained him. Back then he was a MANIAC for a game of fetch!"

That gave me a brilliant idea! "Hey! Let's find a ball!" I said excitedly. "I'm sure there's a few in this Dumpster!"

Normally, Erin would have said, "Max, NOW is a really BAD time to play catch with a dog!"

But I didn't have to explain my master plan to her. She was all in! Even Thumper bounced around the Dumpster, joining in our search.

"Got one!" Erin cried after a minute.

And just in time, too! That police officer's voice seemed to be getting louder again.

Erin handed me a rubber ball a teacher must have confiscated from some poor kid. Well, now it belonged to Thumper.

I held the ball in front of Thumper's face. "Wanna play fetch, buddy?" I said, tossing it over the wall.

Hey, I'm not trying to brag, but that ball sailed across the parking lot like a death ray from the Incredible Hawk's bionic talon!

"Good thinking, Max!" Erin gushed.

"Whoa, boy!" we heard the officer exclaim. "WHERE are you going?! Come back here!"

I jumped out of the Dumpster, crept over to the door, and cautiously peeked out.

In the distance I saw the officer chasing Thumper across the parking lot.

"Whatcha got?" he finally said. "A BALL?! Is that what you wanted from that Dumpster, you CRAZY dog?!"

I motioned for Erin to join me.

"We can't play catch now, boy! Sarge will put BOTH of us in the DOGHOUSE!" The officer chuckled at his own joke. "Come on. They want us to do a sweep inside."

We watched silently as the man and his dog walked toward the school building.

However, when the dog suddenly stopped, looked back in our direction, and whimpered, my heart started to pound again.

Luckily, the officer just whistled and tugged at the dog's collar to get him to heel.

"Wow! You were AWESOME, Max!" Erin gushed again. "I'm sorry I totally freaked out!"

"No problem! Actually, I freaked out too."

Erin and I kind of stared at each other for a few seconds, and then we smiled and blushed.

Hey, I could have stood there staring at her all night. Even with cottage cheese in her hair, she was still amazing ~~and cute~~! Can you blame me?

"Come on! Let's get out of here while we can!" I exclaimed.

I didn't know which I felt more—happy or relieved.

I had been trapped at my school for more than EIGHT HOURS!

And FINALLY! My trusty sidekick and I were heading HOME!

SWEET!!

5. PANIC IN THE PARKING LOT

We snuck out of the enclosure and into the parking lot.

It was almost completely empty except for the police cars and an old truck.

We were finally FREE! FREE! FREE! WOO-HOO!!

Okay, I LIED!! We weren't quite free . . . YET.

The parking lot was HUGE, and anyone passing by could see us.

Including all the police officers inside the school near windows.

It felt like we were crossing a minefield in a video game or something. I'm not gonna lie, it was very STRESSFUL and very SCARY!

We had made it almost halfway across the parking lot when three officers strolled out of the school.

We made a mad dash for the nearest tree. Then we ducked behind it and held our breath....

ERIN AND ME, DUCKING BEHIND A TREE!

This reminded me of the time my parents caught me SECRETLY shipping my baby brother, Oliver, to my uncle Chuck's house in Michigan....

In my defense, I was only seven. I was sick of his nonstop screaming and him slobbering on my toys.

I don't have the slightest idea why my mom and dad were so upset with me. I cut air holes into the box so he could breathe and tossed in his favorite blankie for the long trip!

Hey! I'm **NOT** a **MONSTER!**

Anyway, that's when I noticed that one of the cops was searching the area with a flashlight, and soon two others joined him.

It was just a matter of time before they discovered US hanging out there in the middle of the parking lot behind a tree.

I started to sweat as they got closer and closer.

"Max, what are we going to do?!" Erin whispered nervously.

I scanned the parking lot for cover. But there was nothing close by except an old truck.

We really didn't have much of a choice. . . .

ERIN AND ME, DIVING INTO THE BACK OF A PARKED TRUCK!

Then we tried our best to hide in the truck's bed under the strange assortment of items.

We almost had heart attacks when two officers walked right up to the truck with flashlights in hand and started talking about who was going to prepare the official incident report.

We just held our breath and tried not to move a muscle. That's when I started to have the most disturbing thoughts. . . .

WHAT if Thumper smelled our scents and happily jumped into the back of the truck with us and playfully dropped his slobbery rubber ball at my feet for me to toss AGAIN?

WHAT if I had to SNEEZE?! The truck WAS very dusty. Just thinking about it made me FEEL like I really had to sneeze. *Don't sneeze! Don't sneeze!*

Finally, the officers sauntered away back toward the school.

WOW! That was close! Thank goodness I didn't . . .

AH! AH! AH-CHOOO!

6. A TRUCKLOAD OF TROUBLE

Erin handed me a tissue for my nose! WHERE do girls get tissues from? Out of thin air?!

Just as quickly as the officers had appeared, they all went back into the school. Phew!

But we didn't DARE leave our hiding place. YET!

"EW! Whose truck is this?" Erin asked as she wrinkled her nose. "It's full of junk!"

I rose up onto my knees and looked around me. "Actually, I don't have the slightest idea who owns it! Maybe a teacher left it here over the weekend for some reason? Probably car trouble."

But if it DID belong to a teacher, I wanted to know which one! There was some seriously WACKY stuff in that pickup truck!!

Obviously, one of our teachers had a serious HOARDING problem and desperately needed help. . . .

ERIN AND ME, GAWKING AT ALL
THE WEIRD STUFF!

Erin and I decided it would be safer to stay in the truck until the police officers cleared out. Then we'd make our way home.

I hid next to a broken toilet while Erin kept watch from behind a dusty Christmas tree.

"Now, that's weird. There are people on top of the roof!" she said, pointing. "LOOK!"

I stared at the top of the building. "Maybe the cops are searching up there or something. But they'd better be careful! The roof is being repaired, and I accidentally fell down that construction chute right into the Dumpster," I said. "I don't see anyone up there now."

"Well, there were three people up there a second ago. I wonder where they went," Erin said, craning her neck. "OMG! What if they fell through the chute and into the Dumpster too?!"

"They'll probably SMELL as BAD as I do!" I said, chuckling at my own witty joke.

Suddenly we heard a loud commotion. At first we thought it was a police officer having a meltdown. . . .

"WHAT WAS I THINKING?! WHO BREAKS INTO A MIDDLE SCHOOL?! THOSE KIDS ARE THE WORST! I SHOULDA KNOWN TUCKER AND MOOSE WOULD BE TOTALLY WORTHLESS!!"

WAIT! Did I just hear the names Tucker and Moose?! Those were two of the MEATHEAD criminals who broke into South Ridge Middle School and TERRORIZED me for HOURS!

And that VOICE! I would NEVER, EVER forget it! It was . . . RALPH!! Ringleader of the MEATHEADS!

HOW did he get away from Tinkerbell, the giant python that was kept in the biology classroom?! HOW did he get past the cops?! And Thumper?!!

WHAT would he do if he saw ME?!!

But there was NO reason to freak out. We were safely hidden in the back of the truck! Right?!

Even if Ralph had somehow gotten past the cops by escaping through the construction chute on the roof and into the Dumpster, the LAST thing he'd want would be to hang around the school. Not when the place was crawling with COPS!

And it wasn't like he was going to walk up to some random truck and check out the weird junk in it. Or maybe he would! He WAS a thief, after all!

Erin and I exchanged worried glances.

"Boss! I'm STARVING!! When are we gonna eat?!" Moose whined.

"I'M starving too, boss! I can't believe that pesky kid RUINED our Mighty Meat Monster pizza! If I ever see him again, he's gonna be SORRY!" Tucker snarled.

"SHUT UP, you CLOWNS! Are you trying to get us arrested?! Can't you see this place is CRAWLING with cops?! Just shut your yaps and keep running!"

When I peeked out, I couldn't believe my eyes. . . .

RALPH, TUCKER, AND MOOSE, RUNNING
ACROSS THE PARKING LOT . . .

. . . RIGHT TOWARD OUR HIDING PLACE!

Okay, NOW it was time for me to FREAK OUT!

Suddenly the doors opened and closed, and the engine started up!!

You're probably thinking Erin and I should have jumped out of the truck before it started moving. But it all happened so quickly, we didn't have time to react.

I was also worried those Neanderthals would see us through that big window in the back of the truck and try to run over us or something.

Erin grabbed my arm, and we stared at each other in HORROR as the truck started to move!

I could not believe our terrible luck!

We were being KIDNAPPED in the back of the truck by three brain-dead, bumbling BURGLARS! And they didn't even know it!

That was just WRONG on so many LEVELS!

Hey, call me a coward, but this was WAY WORSE than being trapped inside a locker or a Dumpster.

It was NEXT-LEVEL terrifying! Like being stuck in a really BAD, NEVER-ENDING NIGHTMARE!...

THE BUNGLING BURGLARS, MAKING A GETAWAY WITH US IN THE TRUCK!

"Max, are you okay?" Erin whispered.

Of course I was NOT okay!! DUH!

"You're, um . . . breathing funny," she added.

NO JOKE! On top of my TOTAL TERROR, I was having an asthma attack! And there's nothing funny about an asthma attack. FOR REAL!

The truck turned out of the school parking lot with a loud screech and swerved onto the main road.

Ralph was ranting like a madman. "The wife's going to STRANGLE me because I missed her mom's birthday! And NOW I'm coming HOME without a GIFT!! I could have given her a brand-new computer from that school! But you two NUMBSKULLS messed it up!"

YIKES! Ralph was taking us HOME with him?!

"Sorry, boss! But that was all MOOSE'S fault!"

"No way, boss! It was all TUCKER'S fault!"

"Just shut your TRAPS! It was both of yers fault!
I'd punch you both in the gut if I wasn't driving this
truck!" Ralph snarled.

"I have an idea, Max!" Erin said. "At some point,
we'll stop at a red light. When we do, let's jump out
of the truck and make a run for it!"

"But what if they see us?" I asked.

I couldn't tell if Erin's face was really green or
if it was a reflection from the Christmas tree she
was lying next to.

"I'd rather risk them seeing us NOW than risk
them seeing us at Ralph's house LATER, right?"
she muttered.

If that was supposed to make me feel better,
it DIDN'T!! The next three minutes were the
longest minutes of my life.

Since it was past midnight with less traffic on the
roads, we kept hitting green lights.

Ralph seemed to be speeding up, not slowing down.

I was starting to believe we'd NEVER get out of that truck ALIVE.

My life flashed before my eyes.

Suddenly Ralph swerved the truck and the tires squealed loudly.

I slammed into Erin, and the Christmas tree fell on top of both of us.

I thought for sure Ralph saw everything in his rearview mirror. But then he yelled, "Look! A drive-through! And it's STILL open! I just got a genius idea!"

I could NOT believe our luck!

Was he REALLY stopping at a drive-through?

I couldn't decide if Ralph was the WORST criminal ever, or the BEST! I mean, if you're on the run from the law, a few double cheeseburgers would definitely help keep up your energy level, right?

"Welcome to Crazy Burger! May I help you?" came a garbled voice on the speaker.

Erin and I looked at each other, and then at Ralph, who was staring at the drive-through menu.

"So, does a TOY come with the Crazy Burger Kiddie Meal?!" he asked. "I need a birthday present for my mother-in-law. She likes pink. Do you got any of those cute little toys in pink?"

"HUH?" the voice said, totally confused.

"Hey, boss! Can I get a Kiddie Meal too? I'm STARVING!" Moose whined.

"Me too, boss! I want the Kiddie Meal with Tricky Chicky Nuggets. It has the best toy!" Tucker said.

"Come on, Erin!" I exclaimed. "Let's get out of here while they're distracted with their Kiddie Meal orders!"

We had to make our leap to freedom! It was now or never!

"On three?" I said, and Erin nodded. I held up one finger, then two, and finally . . . THREE!

I think we both must have gotten a HUGE rush of adrenaline or something, because we frantically scrambled out of the back of that truck FAST!

Like two very desperate kids being accidentally KIDNAPPED by three VERY DANGEROUS, CRAZY FELONS.

Wait a minute!

We WERE two very desperate kids being accidentally KIDNAPPED by three VERY DANGEROUS, CRAZY FELONS!

What an AMAZING coincidence!

Then we ran to the front of Crazy Burger and dived into some bushes. We lay there in shock, trying to catch our breath.

There must have been a vent nearby blowing air from inside the restaurant, because we started to smell delicious burgers!

Within minutes both of our stomachs were growling like garbage disposals.

Grumble-grumble! Grumble-grumble!

I sighed and looked at Erin.

I was dying to pull a Moose-'n'-Tucker impression and obnoxiously whine, "BOSS, I'M STARVING!! Can't I at least go inside and get a Kiddie Meal? PLEEEASE?!"

But before I could ask, Erin rolled her eyes and shot me a dirty look. "No, MAX! Just . . . NO! Don't even THINK about it!"

DANG, girl! Can't a bro get a burger around here?!

Now I totally understood why so many superheroes work ALONE!

I'm just SAYING!!

8. NIGHT RIDERS ROCK!

We waited until Ralph got his order and pulled back onto the street. Then we raced down the alley next to the restaurant and started walking.

"Well, I think we should get you home first, Erin! So, where do you live?" I asked.

Erin and I were fairly new friends at school, so I'd never been to her house before.

"I live on Windy Hollow Court near Bentbrook Drive. We're probably about two miles away," she answered.

In spite of the disastrous evening, part of me was happy that the night wasn't quite over yet. I'd get to walk Erin home!

"We need to make a left here to get to your house, correct?" I asked.

I stepped toward the street, but Erin yanked me back into the alley. "What if they see us?!"

I looked out at the empty street. "WHO?!"

"The POLICE! Once they finish up at the school, they'll probably cruise around, looking for suspects."

YIKES! Erin was TOTALLY right!! And we didn't exactly blend into the night.

My ~~ice princess costume~~ superhero suit was made out of the reflective material cyclists wear that practically glows in the dark! I was like a huge billboard saying HEY, POLICE! I'M RIGHT HERE! COME ARREST ME NOW!!

"So how are we going to get home?!" I asked.

"VERY CAREFULLY!" Erin said. "Let's go!"

We traveled at a snail's pace, hiding behind trees and ducking into the shadows whenever a car passed.

After about two blocks we were passing a secondhand store that had assorted items sitting in front on the sidewalk.

"Hey, Erin! Take a look at this stuff! It's FREE!"...

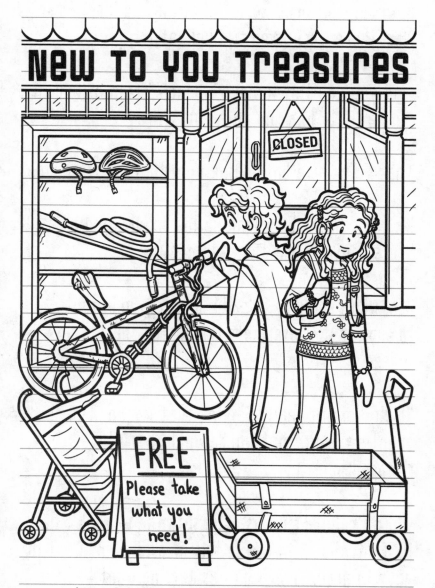

WE LOOK AT SOME FREE STUFF!

I noticed a rusty blue bike with a busted seat.
However, the tires were full of air and looked okay.
Plus, there were even two helmets!

"Did you see this wooden wagon?" Erin asked.
"It's a little beat up, but still sturdy."

That's when we both came up with a creative idea.

We could hook the wagon up to the bike and be at
Erin's house in less than ten minutes.

"So, who's going to ride the bike? Do you want
to flip for it? Loser gets the busted seat!" Erin
teased.

"Well, I'm not really feeling that wagon. The
splinters from that wood could be brutal,"
I teased back.

What a relief Erin was okay with the wagon! It was
MY fault that Erin was in this mess. I didn't want to
have to argue over who was getting what.

"OKAY! I'll take the raggedy wagon. You get the busted bike!" She grinned.

We looked around and found an old jump rope on a bookshelf.

We tied the wagon to the back of the bike, and we were finally ready to roll!

The broken bicycle seat was a little tricky.

It wasn't that bad as long as I was sitting on it. But if I stood up, it would flop over at a weird angle.

Then I'd have to stop and adjust the seat again, which was pretty annoying.

I finally got the hang of it, and soon we were gliding quietly down the sidewalk with my cape flapping in the wind, almost like I was flying!

It was actually kind of COOL! . . .

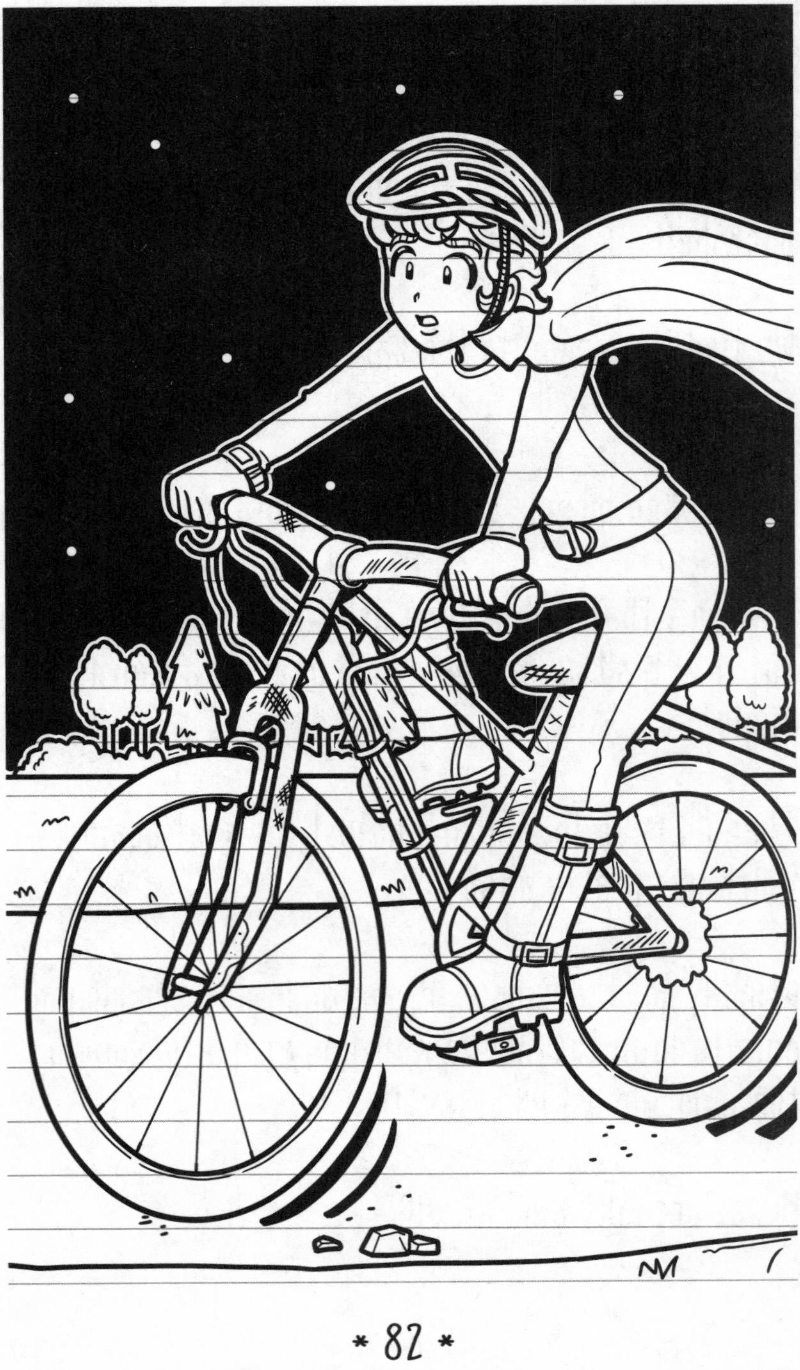

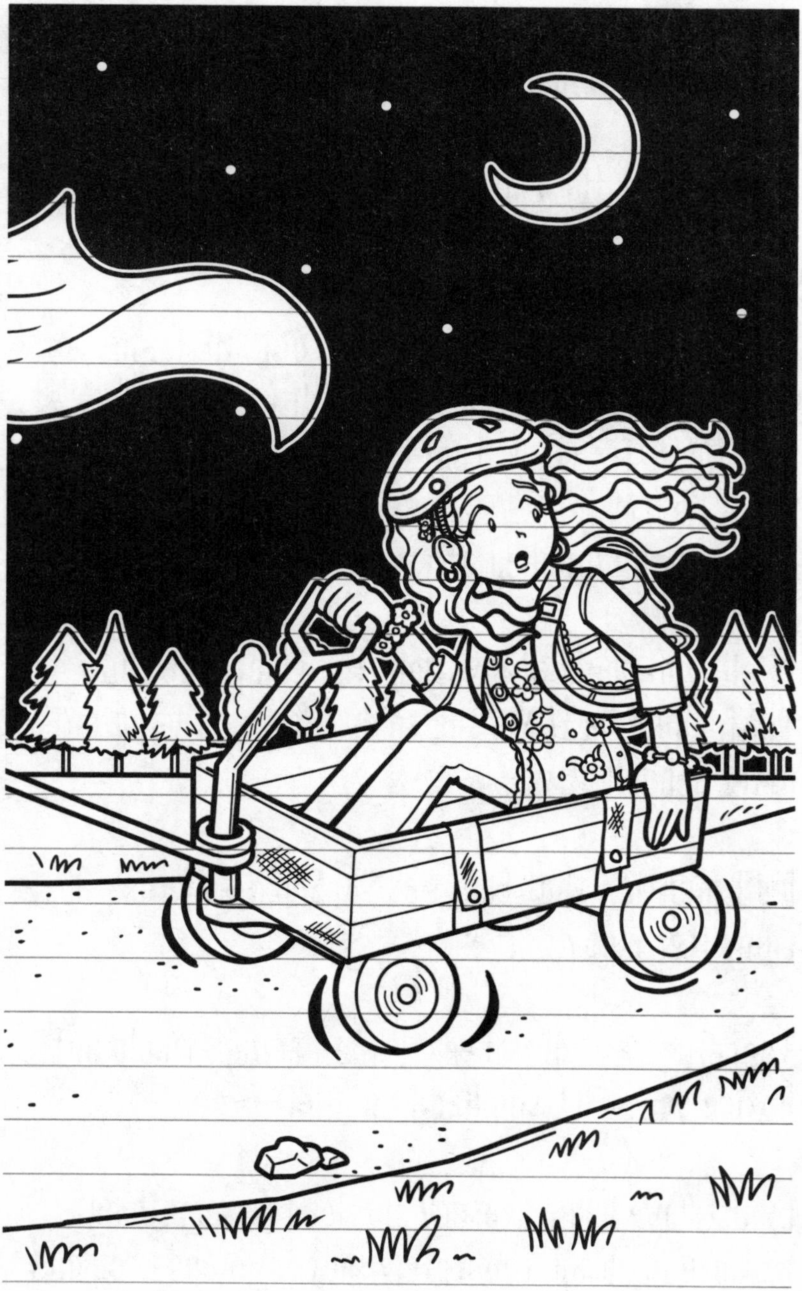

Finally, we reached Erin's house! I was surprised it was just a few blocks from mine.

"Thanks for the ride home, Max." Erin smiled. "That was A LOT of fun!"

"No problem! Thank YOU for rescuing ME from the Dumpster." I smiled back. "Unfortunately, that WASN'T a lot of fun!"

She actually laughed at my little joke! SWEET!!

"Well, you could always join the computer club. THAT would be FUN!" she said. "We could hang out after school!"

Did I mention that Erin was PRESIDENT of the computer club?

There was a slight breeze, and I couldn't help but notice she STILL smelled AMAZING!

I must have had a sensory overload or something, because my brain completely shut down and I couldn't think of anything else to say. It was SO quiet, I could actually hear the crickets chirping. . .

"LOSER!"

"LOSER!"

"LOSER!"

"LOSER!"

"LOSER!"

Okay, the "LOSER" part was probably just my ~~extreme insecurity~~ vivid imagination.

I needed to say something . . . **ANYTHING!**

"So, Erin, has anyone ever told you that you have a really cool, um . . . mailbox? Ours is old and crappy, but my dad is too cheap to buy a new one!"

Of all the great things about her, I could NOT believe I had just complimented her MAILBOX!

"Actually, I think it came with the house. But thanks," Erin answered as we both stared at her mailbox.

"So, Erin, I, um . . . want to apologize for ruining your ice princess costume. My clothes got messed up, and it was kind of an emergency. I'll pay you for it!"

"NO WAY! Max, you put that costume to better use than I EVER could have! It's weird, but it kind of gives you this . . . SUPERHERO vibe! Especially with those great boots! You actually look pretty AWESOME!"

I AM NOT LYING!

She actually said that to me!

For a moment I thought my head was going to EXPLODE from my super-inflated EGO!

"WOW! You REALLY think so?! The whole SUPERHERO thing NEVER crossed my mind! AT ALL!" I lied. "But thanks for the compliment!"

Then we both smiled and kind of stared at each other like they do in all those teen movies my older sister is OBSESSED with. . . .

ERIN AND ME, HANGING OUT
IN FRONT OF HER HOUSE

Suddenly a light flicked on inside Erin's house!

FOR REAL!! It was NOT my night!! DANG!!

"OMG! I better get inside!" Erin exclaimed as she turned and bolted up the driveway.

"Is that your PARENTS?! I hope you're not in even BIGGER trouble!" I said, feeling really guilty again.

"Don't worry! That light is my brother's room. He's probably just grabbing a midnight snack. Thanks again for the ride home. Good night, Max!"

Then she opened the front door and waved.

"Sure! Thank YOU for . . . everything!" I said. "And . . ."

But she disappeared inside and closed the door behind her before I could finish my sentence.

". . . good night, Erin!" I muttered to myself.

I suddenly felt like a total WEIRDO standing there on the sidewalk in the middle of the night, staring at Erin's house on a busted bike pulling a raggedy wagon.

WAIT! I AM that total WEIRDO!

Soon I saw a second light flick on in the house.

I guessed that it was probably Erin's room. Unless it was... HER PARENTS' ROOM?!!!!

OH, CRUD! What if her dad saw me out here?!

Any second now he could fling open the front door and chase me around the block with a broom or something.

SORRY! But Max C. was NOT going down like that!!

I took off on my busted bike with that raggedy wagon and quickly disappeared into the night.

9. MY DESPERATE DITCH AND DASH!

I pedaled toward home as fast as I could.

I wasn't that worried about my neighbors seeing me, since all of them were asleep by now.

The challenge was going to be slipping inside my house without being noticed. And then acting like everything was TOTALLY NORMAL in the morning.

You know, like I hadn't been up most of the night hanging out with COPS and ROBBERS!

I was almost home. And soon this whole nightmare would be over!!

Since I was EXHAUSTED, I decided to take a shortcut across our neighbor's lawn.

Mr. Howell is the head of the neighborhood association. He's eighty-two years old and meaner than a junkyard dog!

He leaves nasty notes taped on our trash bins if my parents leave them out an hour past pickup.

And once he called the police to report a "very loud and out-of-control party with excessive drinking!"

It was my little brother's birthday, and a group of four-year-olds were playing Duck, Duck, Goose in our backyard and sipping juice boxes. GO FIGURE!!

My mom says Mr. Howell is lonely and just wants to be invited to our social events.

Anyway, if he caught me dragging a busted bike and a raggedy wagon across his PERFECTLY MANICURED LAWN, I was VERY sure he'd have a complete MELTDOWN.

I was sneaking across his yard when I heard his front door open.

Mr. Howell came rushing out of his house in his pajamas, SCREAMING his head off. . . .

MR. HOWELL, SCREAMING AT ME!

At first I froze like a deer in headlights. Then I panicked!

I am NOT proud of the fact that I DITCHED my busted bike and raggedy wagon on Mr. Howell's beautiful front lawn.

But I really didn't have a choice.

If he actually called the police, they'd interrogate me under a hot light like they do on TV. In less than thirty seconds, I'd totally CONFESS I was at school most of the night.

It would be a DISASTER!

Erin would HATE ME!

The cops would ARREST ME!

And my parents would KILL ME!

It was SO much easier to just leave my stuff there, jump over the fence into my yard, and disappear!

Mr. Howell put that stupid fence up a year ago for "more privacy." I thought it was a good idea.

I mean, it's NOT like I WANT to watch him sunbathing!!

The dude is so old and wrinkled, he looks like a human-sized PRUNE in swim trunks, sunglasses, and flip-flops....

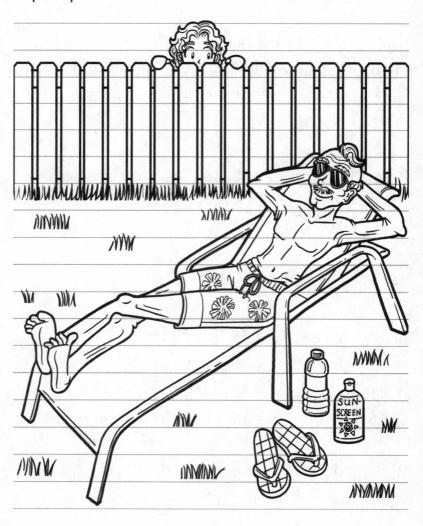

Anyway . . . FINALLY, I WAS HOME!!

HOME SWEET HOME!

I had never been so happy and excited to be at my house!

For some reason, I felt like a completely different person.

It seemed like only yesterday THUG had locked me inside my locker and totally RUINED my life!

WAIT! That WAS only yesterday!

But it felt like WEEKS!

Now I'm STRONGER and SMARTER! I could challenge THUG to a one-on-one basketball game and totally kick his BUTT!

I had successfully survived the past twenty-four hours and made a new friend! That made me a WINNER in the GAME OF LIFE. . . .

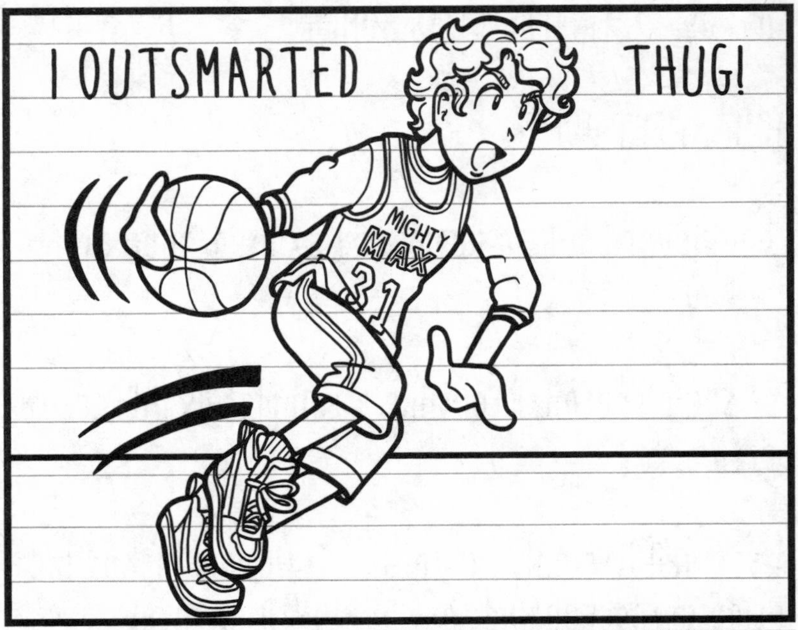
I OUTSMARTED THUG!
MIGHTY MAX 31

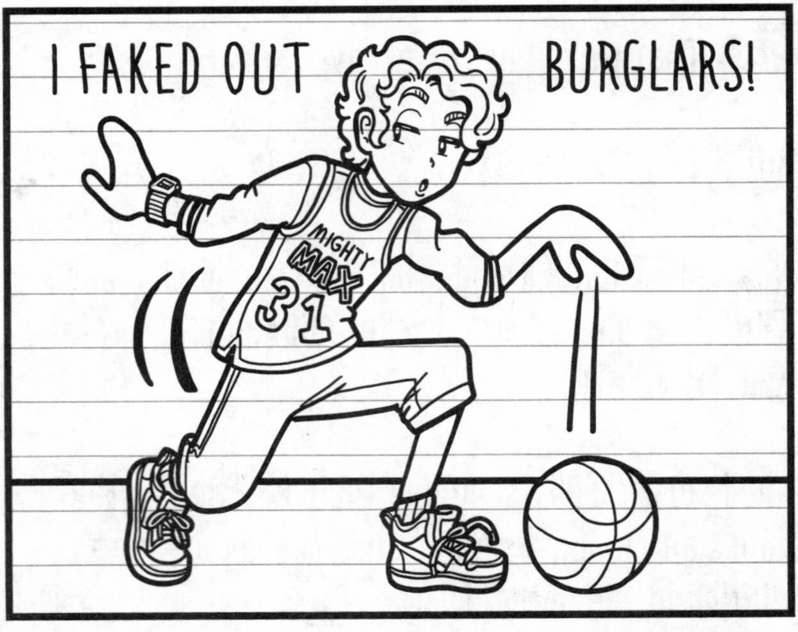
I FAKED OUT BURGLARS!
MIGHTY MAX 31

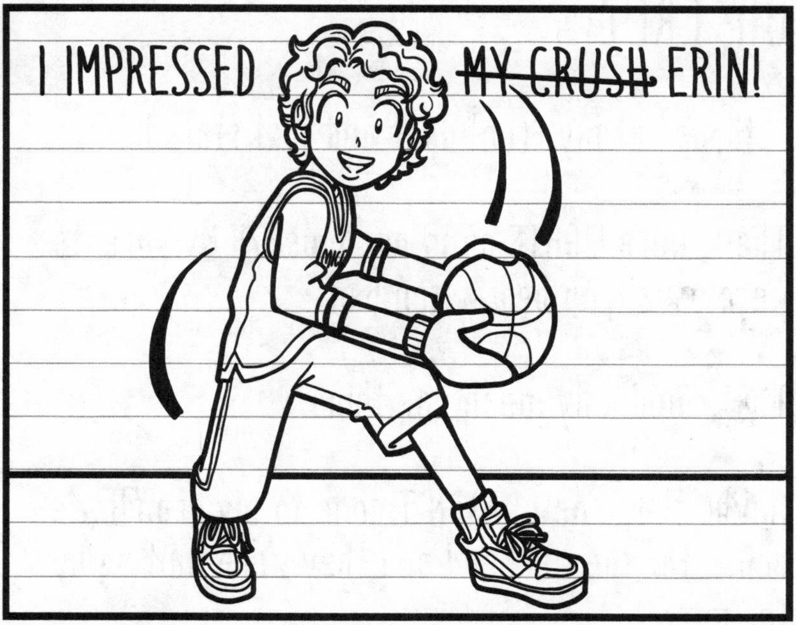
I IMPRESSED ~~MY CRUSH~~ ERIN!
MIGHTY

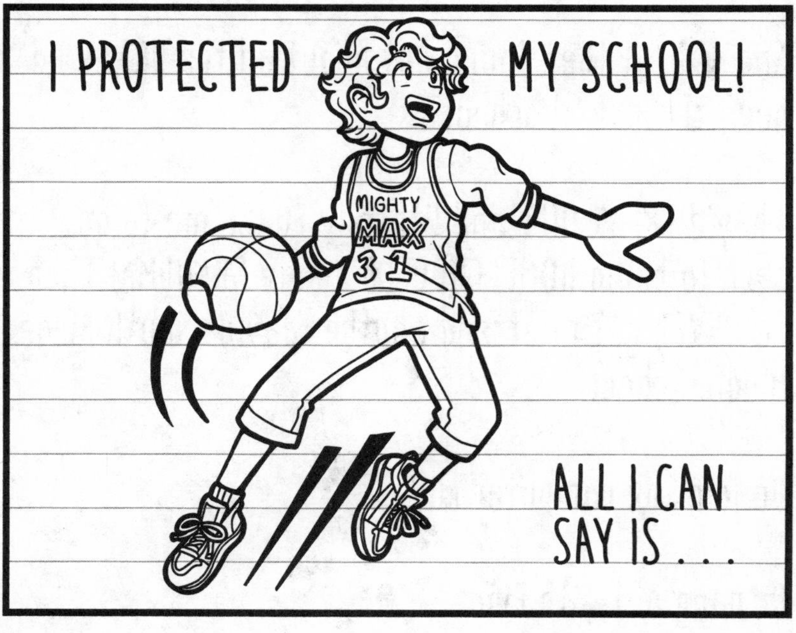
I PROTECTED MY SCHOOL!
MIGHTY
MAX
31
ALL I CAN
SAY IS . . .

OH, CRUD!

I stopped at my front door and just stared!

There were LIGHTS on in my house?!! My parents were usually in bed by ten p.m.

That could only mean one thing. . . .

Maybe they knew I HADN'T gone to my grandma's house for the weekend and they were waiting up for me!

And what if they found out about all the DRAMA I'd been through at school?

They'd FREAK OUT and literally FORCE me to go back to being HOMESCHOOLED by my GRANDMA! Then I'd NEVER get to attend another day at South Ridge Middle School.

Or join the computer club.

Or hang out with Erin.

MY.
LIFE.
WAS.
OVER!!!

10. I SNEAK IN AND FREAK OUT!

Okay, this was bad. **REALLY BAD!!**

What if my parents were waiting up for me?! I was pretty much DEAD!!

I should have just stayed in the back of that truck and taken my chances with Ralph, Moose, and Tucker!

I didn't have a choice but to ring the doorbell, spill my guts, and beg my parents for mercy. Erin would get in big trouble too, and I'd probably never see her again.

I felt like I was drowning in a **HUGE** wave of despair.

Finally it was GAME OVER!

SORRY! But Max C. wasn't going down like that!!

In the past twenty-four hours, I'd managed to evade a bully, three burglars, a half dozen police officers, and a senile, lawn-obsessed elderly neighbor.

I'd escaped from a locker, boiler room, ventilation system, boys' bathroom, Dumpster, and more.

I'd successfully made the treacherous trek from school to home in the middle of the night ~~(and I STILL had a HUGE adrenaline rush from that romantic moonlit ride with my crush, Erin)~~. So I was NOT about to give up now that I was less than fifty feet away from my BEDROOM! FOR REAL!

If Erin could sneak OUT of her house to rescue me, then I could at least sneak INTO my house to save my butt. I just had to figure out how to do it.

That's when I remembered that the lock on the family room window was loose. My mom had been nagging my dad to fix it for months.

I could sneak in through that window and make it up to my room without my parents seeing me.

Then I'd just pretend I'd come home from my grandma's house earlier that evening and hung out in my bedroom playing video games until bedtime.

PROBLEM SOLVED!!

I crept along the side of the house to the family room window and peeked inside.

A light was on in the hallway. But the room itself was totally dark except for a dim night-light or something that I'd never noticed before.

I slowly raised the window and cautiously stuck my head inside the room to listen for my parents.

Suddenly the lamp next to the window clicked on! It was so glaringly bright that I was briefly blinded.

When my eyes finally adjusted, I gasped in horror!

I was face-to-face with the UGLIEST CREATURE I'd ever seen in my entire life!

It looked like a half-zombie, half-alien MONSTER from my worst nightmare! It had slimy, oatmeal-colored skin and huge, spongy rolls of pink flesh protruding out of its head!! . . .

I SCREAMED! It SCREAMED! Then we BOTH SCREAMED in absolute TERROR!!!...

ME, FREAKING OUT AT
THE HIDEOUS CREATURE LURKING IN
THE FAMILY ROOM!!

We just stared at each other and screamed hysterically until I noticed that the monster was holding my sister Megan's hot-pink glitter cell phone.

This meant one of two things.

The monster had EATEN my sister, had STOLEN HER PHONE, and was WEARING HER ROBE!

(What WEIRDO would STEAL someone's phone and WEAR their clothes?! Well, other than . . . ME!)

OR the monster **WAS** my SISTER!

Apparently, Megan was doing another one of her trendy BEAUTY treatments that ironically made her face look BABOON-BUTT UGLY!

What could I say?! MY BAD!!

I know my OWN sister shouldn't have freaked me out like that! But can you blame me? She looked absolutely BANANAS!! That oatmeal face mask was beyond GROSS!

It looked like she'd thrown up her breakfast cereal and then decided to smear it on her face. EWW!!

Megan got all up in my face like bad breath.

"Shut up, you birdbrain!" she hissed. "What are you trying to do, wake up Mom and Dad so they'll come down here and ground us and take away our phones?! And WHO are YOU supposed to be? That chick from the *FROZEN* movie?!"

Then she flopped back on the couch, stared at her phone, and started texting madly like I wasn't even there.

I just rolled my eyes. Then I hoisted myself up through the window and tumbled onto the floor. I closed the window and glared at my sister.

"Well, Sleeping Beauty, isn't it a little past your bedtime?! And, from the looks of it, you could use some beauty sleep. Like, thirty years' worth! Because right now you look like a giant-sized, super-UGLY oatmeal cookie!"

Megan suddenly stopped texting.

She sniffed in my direction and wrinkled her nose.

"OMG, Max!" she muttered. "You smell worse than usual. What did you do, roll around in a pile of rotting garbage?"

Okay, THAT was the last straw! I had just SAVED South Ridge Middle School! I was a HERO! I should be getting a MEDAL for my courage! NOT lame INSULTS from my sister!!

"Maybe I SHOULD wake Mom and Dad," I shot back. "You're violating their cell phone rule!"

Megan smirked. "I'm not allowed to be on my phone with friends late at NIGHT. They never said anything about the wee hours of the MORNING!"

WHATEVER!!

I just hoped Megan stayed on her stupid phone until that thick CRUD on her face dried and hardened like CEMENT. Then she wouldn't be able to OPEN that BIG, FAT MOUTH of hers anymore!

I trudged up the stairs to my bedroom, suddenly exhausted.

It had been the longest DAY of my PATHETIC little life. I was DYING to just crawl into my bed fully clothed.

But Megan was right. Unless I wanted my bedroom (and possibly the entire upstairs) to smell like a Dumpster, I needed to do SOMETHING about that RANK STANK!

I carefully pulled my dad's comic book out of my boot. I needed to return it to his collection ASAP since he didn't know I had borrowed it.

But first I peeled off my dirty clothes and left them in a big smelly pile on the floor. Only a long, hot bath could soak through the layers of filth and stench on my skin.

And since Megan was GRIPING about my really bad

smell, I was SURE she wouldn't mind me ~~stealing~~ borrowing her zesty Sunshine Citrus Beach bath and body gift basket that she'd gotten for her birthday. Soon I was feeling clean, happy, and relaxed. . . .

ME, CHILLAXING IN THE TUB!!

I was actually inspired to write a rap!...

WASH IT OFF!
(A RAP WRITTEN BY COOL MAX C.)

Sometimes you reach
the end of your rope.
Everything's wrong.
You're losing hope.

You're covered in slime
and mystery meat.
You want to give up.
Admit defeat.

You're unappreciated,
filthy, and tired.
And all you got are
the bruises you've acquired.

Just hop in the tub.
Wash away life's crud!
Just wash it off!
WASH IT OFF!

Sometimes you fail.
You flunk a big test.
You don't make the team
although you tried your best.

Kids in the hall
are laughing at you.
Because toilet paper
is stuck on your shoe.

Wash away bad vibes.
Don't own 'em any longer.
You'll be nice and clean
and A LOT stronger!

Jump in the shower.
You've got the power
to wash it off!
JUST WASH IT OFF!

I had no friends.
My life was sad.
That bully was brutal.
The haters were bad.

I was stuck in the muck
inside a filthy DUMPSTER!
Facing my fear that was
as scary as a MONSTER!

I didn't give up.
I fought the fight.
I hung in there.
My future is bright!

So when life is crappy,
just smile and be happy.
You can wash it off.
JUST WASH IT OFF!

I don't mean to brag, but I know I've got serious
SKILLZ!!

My rap summed up exactly how I felt about
my life.

I was relieved this NIGHTMARE was finally over
and tomorrow everything was going to be back
to normal.

I actually kind of missed my old, boring life!

Suddenly I felt SO tired, I could barely keep my eyes open.

I had this nagging feeling there was something really important I was supposed to do, but I couldn't remember what it was.

So I decided to deal with all that tomorrow after I'd gotten some sleep. I slipped into my pj's and climbed into my soft, comfortable bed.

I was happy to be back at MY house, in MY bedroom, sleeping in MY bed. But, more than anything, I was happy I'd made it out of my middle school ALIVE and Erin had been there to help me.

I was physically, mentally, and emotionally exhausted. In less than sixty seconds I had fallen into a very deep sleep.

11. PLEASE, GET OUT OF MY ROOM!

I opened my eyes in a panic and stared at the ceiling.

It was already morning, and sunlight flooded my room.

BANG-BANG! BANG-BANG!

It sounded like someone was hammering nails into my skull.

With a sledgehammer!

I groaned, rolled over, and pulled my pillow over my head.

EWW!! WHAT was that horrible odor?!

It smelled like a skunk had sprayed my room and then crawled under my bed and had a bad case of diarrhea!

BANG-BANG! BANG-BANG!

Every nerve in my body was FREAKING OUT!!!

"MAX!! Are you awake? Megan told us you came home last night instead of staying at Grandma's house."

I lifted my pillow and stared at the door.

It was my dad. WHY was he banging on my door like that?! Give me a break!

WAIT! MY DAD WAS AT MY BEDROOM DOOR?!!

I sat bolt upright as my heart pounded in my chest!

YIKES! DAD'S COMIC BOOK!!

I'd meant to put it back in his desk drawer last night, but I was so tired, I had totally forgotten!

Now it was sitting on my shelf in plain sight!

I scrambled out of bed, grabbed the comic, and looked desperately around my room.

WHERE COULD I HIDE IT?!

"Max?! Are you in there?!" my dad asked, concerned.

I frantically shoved the comic into my math textbook.

Just as my dad turned the door handle, I realized my filthy costume and the rest of my clothes were STILL lying in a pile on the floor, exactly where I'd left them last night.

So THAT'S why my room smelled like a skunk!

In a panic, I dove into the pile and somehow shoved the entire thing under my bed in seconds. Then I nervously sat on the edge of my bed with my arms and legs crossed, trying NOT to look as GUILTY as I felt.

I have no idea how I had missed my smelly boots! I was trying to kick them under my bed with my foot when my dad walked in. . . .

ME, TRYING NOT TO LOOK GUILTY!

Yeah, Dad! NOW I'm awake! Thanks to YOU. But DANG! Can't a growing teen get some sleep around here?!!

But I didn't actually say any of that snarky stuff to my dad. Hey, I don't have a DEATH wish!!

"Since you won't be at your grandmother's this weekend as planned, I could use your help cleaning out the garage," he explained.

Suddenly he stopped talking, sniffed the air, and looked concerned.

"Speaking of cleaning, Max, your room is getting a little . . . um, RIPE!"

"Yeah, I know! I'm going to clean it today."

"Good idea!" he answered. Then he wrinkled his nose and scanned my room like he was trying to figure out where that smell was coming from.

I jumped up and escorted my dad toward the door.

"As a matter of fact, I think I'm going to clean my room right NOW! So why don't you just go downstairs and relax? Maybe get a cup of coffee," I said, closing the door behind him.

"Okay, Max. I'll see you in the garage in ten minutes!" Dad yelled through the door.

TEN MINUTES?! How was I going to get dressed AND get rid of that pile of smelly clothes in only ten minutes?!

I put on my favorite shirt and jeans, then rushed down to the kitchen. My mom was already fixing breakfast.

"Good morning, dear!" She smiled. "I'm sorry things didn't work out with your grandma."

The plan was that I'd stay at my grandma's house to look after her furry little Yorkshire terror terrier, Creampuff, while she and her friends went to the Westchester Knitting Convention for the weekend.

Grandma was even going to pay me to basically sit around and play video games at her house all day. But she'd canceled at the last minute because it was supposed to rain. It didn't rain! Not one drop!

"No problem, Mom," I said as I grabbed a trash bag from under the kitchen sink. I had just enough time to dispose of the evidence in my room before helping my dad clean the garage.

"What's up, Max? I'm really surprised YOU'RE already awake!" Megan said.

I jumped. Where had she come from?!

She eyeballed me like she was a hungry snake and I was her next meal. "Max, you look super tired. What time did you go to bed last night?"

I stared her down. Did she actually think she could intimidate me?!

She had NO IDEA what I had been through in the last twenty-four hours!

Two could play this little game! Megan started it, but I was going to finish it!

And if I was going down, she was going with me!! . . .

I FEEL GREAT, MEGAN! BUT YOU LOOK EXHAUSTED! SO, WHAT TIME DID **YOU** GO TO BED LAST NIGHT?!

ME, INTERROGATING MEGAN ABOUT **HER** BEDTIME LAST NIGHT!

At first she glared at me. But she quickly plastered a fake smile across her face because Mom was watching.

"Actually, I DON'T remember!" Megan shrugged. Then she narrowed her eyes at me and slunk away.

"Five minutes, Max!" my dad called from the garage.

I raced up the stairs to my room, pulled the smelly clothing out from under my bed, and stuffed everything into the garbage bag.

I felt bad throwing Erin's costume away since she had made it especially for the school play. And even though the play had been canceled, she probably could have used it for something else. But, thanks to me, now it wasn't fit to wear to a mud-wrestling contest!

I took the bag out to the garbage bin on the curb, tossed it inside, and slammed the bin shut.

I immediately felt a sense of relief.

Now there was even LESS evidence that could implicate me in that investigation at my school.

I was about to run back into the house, grab a granola bar, and help my dad, when I heard a loud commotion coming from next door.

I turned around to see our grumpy neighbor, Mr. Howell, striding toward our house.

And he did NOT look happy! But that wasn't even the worst part.

He was dragging a busted bike and a raggedy wagon.

Actually, MY busted bike and raggedy wagon!

I just FROZE and stared at him.

I had been awake for LESS than fifteen minutes, and already my day was turning into a complete DISASTER!!

And THAT was just WRONG on so many levels!

12. SORRY, BUT MY DAD IS NOT HOME

Thank goodness I hadn't eaten breakfast yet!

Seeing Mr. Howell with the bike and wagon Erin and I had used in our getaway made me feel SICK!

My stomach was doing so many flip-flops, I thought I was going to THROW UP in that garbage bin.

I had just gotten rid of all the clothing I'd worn last night. And now Mr. Howell was dragging over MORE evidence that could RUIN MY LIFE!

GIVE ME A BREAK! This day could NOT get any worse!

I turned and quickly walked up the driveway back to the garage.

I had already come up with a plan to avoid Mr. Howell. And it was brilliant!

I was going to close the overhead garage door. Lock the front door. Refuse to answer the phone or the doorbell. And not allow any of my family members to leave the house. For TWO MONTHS! By that time, Mr. Howell would have completely forgotten about us and started to HARASS some other poor family and make THEIR lives miserable!

Unfortunately, I wasn't able to close the garage door because a broom was in the way. DANG!!

Mr. Howell was standing there in the driveway, and I could tell he was mad. "Hello, Max! I really NEED to speak with your father! It's an EMERGENCY!"

Yeah, right! What Mr. Howell really NEEDED was to MIND HIS OWN BUSINESS! I'm just saying!

My dad had just stepped inside the house a minute earlier to use the bathroom. But Mr. Howell didn't know that. So I implemented emergency plan B! . . .

"Um . . . I'm really sorry, Mr. Howell, but my dad isn't home right now! I'll tell him you stopped by."

Yes! Emergency plan B was to LIE like a RUG!

"Well, this is VERY important! WHERE did he go and WHEN will he be back?!" Mr. Howell asked.

"I think he went to . . . the . . . um . . . hardware store."

"Are you sure? It doesn't open on Saturdays until ten a.m.," Mr. Howell said, glancing at his watch. "That's an HOUR from now!"

"Actually, he went to the, um . . . CupCakery bakery! It opens early. But he'll probably run errands after that. He could be gone for quite a while."

"Should I come back in a few hours?" he asked.

"How about . . . um, next . . . Friday? Maybe. I'm sorry, but he's REALLY busy," I explained.

"FRIDAY?!" Mr. Howell gasped. "Are you sure?! Well, okay then. I guess I'll try again next week!"

I could NOT believe my plan had actually worked!! Mr. Howell was about to turn and leave when . . .

MY DAD, COMING BACK FROM
THE BATHROOM!

Things could NOT get any worse! But, for some reason, the normally grumpy Mr. Howell was in a really chatty mood.

"Well, Crumbly, I'm glad you're back. I was just about to leave. Your son here told me where you went. It's actually one of my favorite places!"

I looked at my dad and shrugged like I didn't have the slightest idea what the guy was talking about.

"Really? Well, what can I say? When you gotta go, YOU GOTTA GO!" Dad chuckled.

"Well, next time let me know. I'll go with you, if you don't mind," Mr. Howell said.

Dad stared at Mr. Howell. "You're joking! Right?!"

Mr. Howell was talking about the BAKERY, but Dad was talking about the BATHROOM. Yes, it was all MY fault! But I only stretched the truth to get rid of Mr. Howell. He was going to SNITCH on me and completely DESTROY my life!

Can you blame me? I was already dealing with a Dumpster load of problems BEFORE he showed up!

I was worried their conversation was going to be a little TWISTED!! . . .

ME, WISHING MR. HOWELL WOULD GO HOME!

This entire FIASCO was SO . . . embarrassing!

"Now, my favorite thing is all the smells! I love the SMELL of that place!" Mr. Howell gushed. "It's also a great place to relax. I always bring a book, magazine, or newspaper to read."

"Well, I have to admit, I've done THAT a few times myself," Dad said, looking a little uncomfortable.

Mr. Howell continued. "Sometimes I just sit in there for hours. Once I accidentally dozed off and almost fell over. I made a HUGE mess! It was nearly impossible to get those brown chocolate stains out of my clothing."

Dad looked totally grossed out. He had no idea Mr. Howell was talking about a chocolate cupcake.

"Anyway," Mr. Howell said, "the next time I go, I'll let you know, and you should do the same. Hey, why don't we invite the ENTIRE neighborhood?!"

Dad cleared his throat loudly. "Listen, Mr. Howell,

it's been nice chatting with you, and thank you for stopping by. But, as you can see, we're right in the middle of cleaning out our garage."

"Well, it's about time! The place is a mess!" Mr. Howell muttered.

"Anyway, I hope you enjoy your bike ride around the neighborhood! Have a nice day!" Dad said.

"This isn't MY bicycle! I'm returning it to YOU! I don't understand why YOUR kids think it's okay to leave their JUNK on my lawn!!" Mr. Howell fumed.

Dad looked at Mr. Howell, at the bike and the wagon, and then at me. "Actually, I've never seen that bike or wagon before today, Mr. Howell. What about you, Max?"

I shrugged and tried not to freak out! "Um . . . they're not mine." (Which was true! Technically, they belonged to the secondhand shop downtown. Right? Or did they become mine the moment I took them out of the free-stuff pile? This was a moral dilemma I did

NOT have the energy to struggle with right then!)

"Oliver's still on training wheels," Dad continued, "and I haven't seen Megan break a sweat in five years. So unless they belong to my wife, I don't know what to tell you."

Mr. Howell looked like his head was going to EXPLODE....

MR. HOWELL WAS NOT HAPPY!

He totally lost it and went into a crazy rant. . . .

"All I know is that this JUNK just mysteriously appeared on MY lawn in the middle of the night! And when I went outside to investigate, I saw a strange person wearing a long silver cape and boots. He flew over the fence and then quickly disappeared through a window at YOUR house! I've already reported the incident to the police."

MR. HOWELL CALLED THE POLICE?!!
This situation could NOT get any worse!

Dad gave me a concerned look and shook his head in disbelief. Did he think Mr. Howell was senile?

"Well! That's quite a story, Mr. Howell. I assure you, no space alien in a silver cape visited our house last night. But thanks for your concern."

I almost felt sorry for the old guy. But notice I said "ALMOST"!

Hey, he'd called the police on ME!! HOW were we

going to clean out our garage if the authorities showed up in helicopters and wrapped yellow crime-scene tape everywhere?...

It was quite obvious my dad felt sorry for our elderly neighbor.

"Listen, Mr. Howell, I understand why you're upset! Maybe we can help. We'd be happy to take this stuff off your hands. Just leave it here with us, and we'll take care of it for you!"

That's when I TOTALLY lost it!

"DAD, NO! THAT'S A REALLY BAD IDEA!" I exclaimed. "WE CAN'T KEEP THAT STUFF HERE! WE'RE, UM . . . TRYING TO CLEAN OUT THE JUNK IN THE GARAGE! NOT COLLECT MORE OF IT! RIGHT?!"

Dad tapped his chin. "Good point, Max! Your mom suggested we donate the items we don't want to that new secondhand shop. They'll sell your stuff and give the money to local charities. I bet if I fix the bike seat and tighten the wagon wheels, they might be useful to someone. Then you and I can drop them off at that shop along with OUR stuff!"

WAIT, WHAT?!!

Did my dad just offer to take the bike and the wagon BACK to the secondhand shop?!!

NO WAY! Now MY head was about to EXPLODE!

I had a million questions!

What if their security camera showed that I had taken them from their FREE pile LATE last night? And what if they asked me WHY I was returning them? In front of my DAD?!!

Or, worse yet, what if the POLICE came to my house, confiscated the bike and wagon as evidence, and then found the clothing I had just tossed in the garbage bin?!

And what if they interviewed the ~~nosy neighbor~~ eyewitness who said he saw a person dressed in that same clothing climb in through OUR window in the middle of the night?!

And what if Mr. Howell picked ME out of a criminal lineup of suspects?!!

You know, like they do on those cop shows on television. . . .

ME, FREAKING OUT AS SUSPECT #3
IN A LINEUP?!

Things could NOT get any worse!

Only this time I REALLY mean it more than all those other times I said it!

I watched silently as Dad and Mr. Howell rolled the bike and wagon into the garage.

Mr. Howell shot me a dirty look as he angrily stomped off, muttering to himself under his breath, "Kids today have no moral compass! They're spoiled rotten! I need to move to a gated community for senior citizens with no kids allowed!"

That's when I decided to go inside and have a nice, big, hot breakfast.

You know, BEFORE the police arrived to arrest me!

I've heard that the food in JAIL is really nasty.

Even nastier than the food in our school cafeteria.

And that's just WRONG on so many levels!

13. UNEXPECTED ~~ALIEN~~ VISITORS?!

I could NOT believe that Mr. Howell had actually called the police on ME!

At first I was a nervous wreck.

Every time a car approached our house, I'd totally panic and think it was the authorities coming to take me away.

But finally I realized I was just being paranoid.

I mean, COME ON!!

Mr. Howell's story was TOTALLY BANANAS!!

What was the likelihood the police would actually show up at MY house to investigate a CRAZY STORY by our elderly neighbor that a strange person in a silver cape had mysteriously appeared, left a pile of JUNK on his front lawn, flown over the fence to our house, and then DISAPPEARED through a window?! . . .

MARS
CLICK

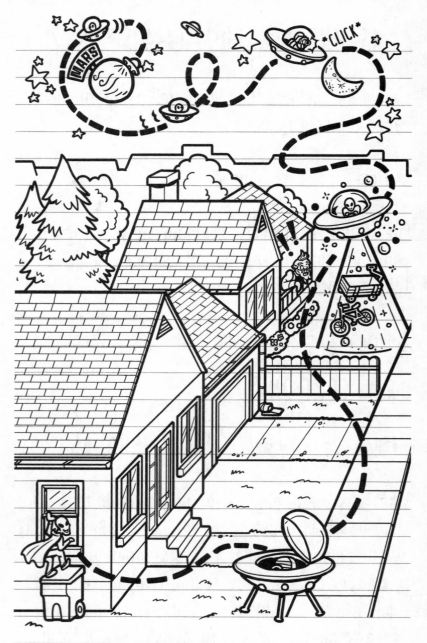

MR. HOWELL'S CRAZY STORY!

Anyway, cleaning out the garage wasn't so bad.
We found some more of my dad's old comic books.

And since they weren't in mint condition, he said
I could have them. SWEET!!

Oliver was hanging out in the backyard with his
friend Brianna, who lives nearby.

I wish I had a sweet little sis like her instead of
a bratty brother who sneaks into my room and
breaks my stuff.

They were noisily playing a make-believe game
called Dinosaurs Invade Baby Unicorn Island. That's
when I suddenly got a GENIUS idea!

Dad was busy filling up a truck he'd borrowed with
stuff for our first trip to the secondhand shop.

But before he could load the bike and wagon,
I asked the munchkins, "Hey! Do you guys want
something cool that will make your game even
more fun? Then check this out!"

They immediately came running. And when they saw the wagon and bike, they FREAKED!!

It didn't matter that the bike was busted and way too big for them, or that the wagon was raggedy. Their imaginations immediately kicked into high gear!

Two six-year-olds and a pile of wood and rusty metal!!

WHAT COULD GO WRONG?!

As they excitedly hauled the bike and wagon to the backyard, Brianna said, "Oliver, your brother is so COOL!"

What can I say? Six-year-olds LOVE me!!

"Okay, Max, here's the plan!" my dad said after I strategically shoved a big box of books into the front passenger seat, where I was supposed to sit. "Since there isn't enough room for you in the front seat, I'll drop off this first load. You can take a break and make the second trip with me."

"Are you sure, Dad?" I asked. "I was really looking forward to helping you unload this stuff...!"

"Thanks, buddy!" Dad smiled and slapped me on the back. "But I think your old man can handle this just fine all by himself."

Actually, my plan was to stall the second trip until dinnertime.

By then the shop would be closed and we could just toss the bike and wagon into the huge donation bins in the parking lot.

NO QUESTIONS ASKED!

When I stepped inside the house, I immediately noticed the sweet aroma of freshly baked chocolate chip cookies.

"Max, can you do me a favor?" my mom said as she headed for the door with her purse and car keys. "I need to run to the grocery store to pick up a few items. Will you keep an eye on Oliver and Brianna in the backyard? I should be back in about thirty minutes. Thanks! Cookies are on the counter!"

"Sure, Mom. And thanks for the snack!" I said.

I poured myself a tall glass of cold milk and grabbed a fistful of cookies. They were warm and gooey and practically melted in my mouth.

I collapsed onto the couch and felt a complete sense of calm for the first time in weeks.

In spite of all the drama I'd been dealing with, surprisingly, EVERYTHING had worked out just FINE!

"Max C. the Man is in complete control!" I smiled.

I was still munching on the chocolaty goodness when the doorbell rang. Who could that be?!

I hopped off the couch and went to look through the peephole. When I saw who was there, I CHOKED on my chocolate chip cookie and quickly opened the door....

I Know. I KNOW!

Max C. the Man was in complete control of his life for less than sixty seconds!

14. DINO BOY AND UNICORN GIRL

I just froze and stared at the officers.

My heart pounded in my chest like a bass drum. I recognized one of them from last night at the middle school.

YIKES!! My worst nightmare was coming true!

"Um . . . okay. But neither of my p-parents are home right now. Is something wr-wrong?" I stammered.

"Well, son, we're trying to figure that out!" Officer Fields said. "There was a break-in and burglary attempt at the middle school last night!"

That's when I almost peed my pants!

It was quite obvious that they were here to arrest me! My life was OVER!

I was already starting to miss my family. Even Megan. And I didn't think THAT was possible!

"We received a call from your next-door neighbor about a possible intruder," Officer Jackson explained. "He said he saw someone enter a window at this address. We wanted to follow up in case it was connected to that middle school break-in. And, of course, we also wanted to make sure YOUR family is safe."

"Thanks, officers! Everyone here is just FINE! My parents should be back soon, so you're welcome to wait. But I also realize you're super busy, and the last thing I'd want is to waste your valuable time on a complaint from a nosy neighbor with an overactive imagination," I said.

The officers exchanged glances and nodded.

Yes! I had just thrown Mr. Howell under the bus!

Hey, it was either HIM or ME!! I was desperate!

Officer Fields handed me his business card and told me to have one of my parents give him a call to verify everything. Then they'd close out the file.

I breathed a HUGE sigh of relief. Maybe I WASN'T going to jail today after all. SWEET!!

They were walking back to their patrol car when Officer Jackson suddenly stopped in her tracks and spun around.

"WAIT! One last thing! Your neighbor said something about finding a bike and a wagon abandoned in his yard. He said he left them here to be given away. If nobody wants them, we can take them down to the station to try to lift some fingerprints. Do you know where they are?"

Did she say "fingerprints"?! WHAT if they found my FINGERPRINTS?! I WAS SO DEAD!!

"Actually, I gave them to my little brother and his friend. They're playing with them in the backyard right now. I'll just explain that you're here to pick them up. They'll get over it!"

I anxiously escorted the police officers to my backyard to seize evidence that would definitely implicate me in the crime at my middle school. But when the officers saw Oliver and Brianna playing, their hearts melted like warm ice cream. . . .

OLIVER AND BRIANNA, HAPPILY PLAYING WITH CRIMINAL EVIDENCE!

"Okay, Oliver and Brianna, these two nice police officers here need to take, er, I mean, borrow your bike and wagon. Okay?!"

"It's NOT a bike! SHE'S a unicorn!!" Brianna protested. "And she's getting dressed up to go to Baby Unicorn Island for her surprise birthday party! She's going to have a PINK unicorn birthday cake with sprinkles on it!"

"And this ISN'T a wagon!" Oliver argued. "It's a dinosaur cave! It's also a tent, a race car, AND a spaceship! ZOOOOM!!"

I tried again. "Sorry, guys, but playtime is over! We need to hand this stuff over to these police officers so they can—!"

"NOW JUST HOLD ON A MINUTE!!" Officer Fields interrupted. "As Jackson explained, we planned to confiscate this stuff ONLY if it was abandoned property. It doesn't look abandoned to me!"

"Me neither!" Office Jackson agreed. "Actually,

we'd need to come back here with a search warrant to take toys from these adorable kids."

"When I was a kid, my favorite toy was a dinosaur too! I called him Danny the Dino!" Officer Fields sniffed. "He was green and one of his eyes was missing. But I didn't care! I really LOVED that little guy!"

"I used to have a bike just like this one when I was a child. I even decorated it with tissue paper flowers. All the kids in the neighborhood would pull them off my bike and blow their noses with them. I really HATED those kids!" Officer Jackson smiled as she reminisced.

"NO WAY are we taking toys from these kids. We're officers, not MONSTERS!" Officer Fields exclaimed. "Besides, we ALL know Mr. Howell down at the station. He's a nice elderly gentleman who's just trying to be helpful. But most of the time he goes way overboard with his one-man neighborhood watch program!"

Officer Jackson seemed highly annoyed too. . . .

Mr. Howell has already made FOUR criminal complaints!

"Really?! FOUR so far this YEAR?" I asked.

Both officers shook their heads.

"FOUR complaints this MONTH?" I guessed.

"NO! Mr. Howell has filed FOUR complaints this WEEK!!" Officer Jackson grumbled.

"Actually, I don't think we'll need that call with your parents after all. We have everything we need to close this file," Officer Fields explained.

"Have a nice day!" Officer Jackson smiled. Then they got into their patrol car and drove away.

I went inside the house and collapsed right in the middle of the living room floor. I felt like my head was going to EXPLODE! For the SECOND time today.

I tried to CHILLAX by reading the comic books my dad had given me. But I was SO exhausted, I must have accidentally fallen asleep or something.

All I remember is hearing a voice, seeing a distorted face, and waking up completely disoriented.

I almost had a PANIC attack until I realized what was going on. . . .

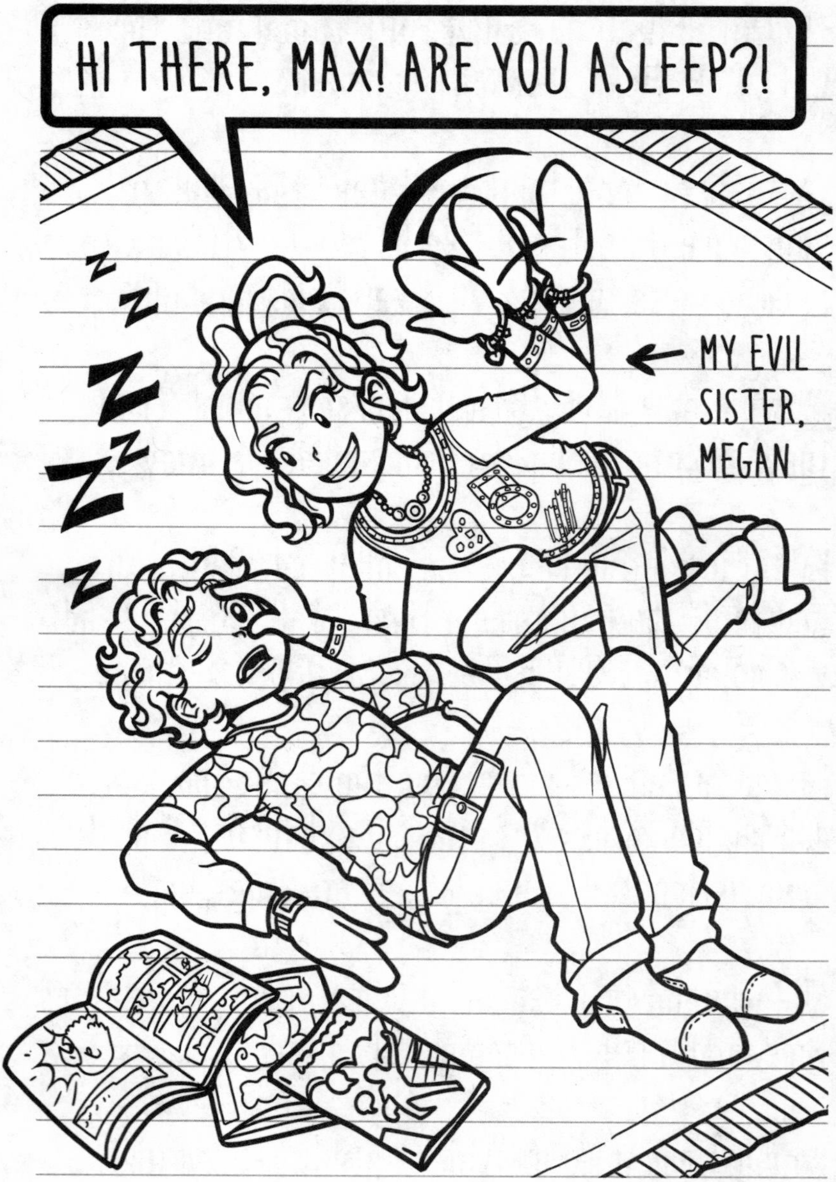
HI THERE, MAX! ARE YOU ASLEEP?!
MY EVIL SISTER, MEGAN

MEGAN, MESSING WITH ME!

"GROW UP, MEGAN!" I yelled at her.

"WHAT?! I was just checking to see if you were still alive! Was someone here? I thought I heard voices."

"You DID! The crazy little VOICES in your HEAD!" I said sarcastically. "They invited you to a sleepover at the city dump! You'd better get going, or you'll be late!"

"Actually, the voices TOLD me to give YOU some mouthwash, BUTT BREATH!" she shot back.

The HATE was REAL!!

But don't get it twisted!

I'd much rather be HOME with my annoying sister driving me NUTS than down at the station with those two police officers, getting a MUG SHOT!

NO JOKE!!

15. BACK TO THE ~~CRIME SCENE~~ SCHOOL

In spite of the long three-day weekend, I still had mixed emotions about returning to school today.

I was DREADING having to face Thug Thurston!

He's the bully who started this whole mess by locking me inside my locker after school on Friday.

Thug has had a problem with me ever since that day I got sick in PE class and accidentally threw up my oatmeal on his expensive athletic sneakers.

It was totally an accident! But it was partially HIS fault too. I didn't SEE him standing there! His body odor is SO bad, it makes your eyes sting and go blurry when you get within ten feet of him.

I was also worried that I'd somehow be implicated in the school break-in.

I'd innocently arrive at school, step off the bus, and then . . .

MY LIFE WOULD BE OVER!!

I could be sent to the principal's office, suspended from school, detained by the police, questioned, arrested, and then thrown in jail, all BEFORE my third-hour class!

But, more than anything, I was DYING to see Erin again! I was really worried about her, but I didn't have her home phone number and there wasn't any other way to contact her.

Her parents had confiscated her LAPTOP late Friday night when they caught her using it (she was talking to ME!) in violation of their rules.

Then I'd accidentally busted her CELL PHONE when I'd fallen off the roof of the school into that DUMPSTER. It was probably STILL in there!

Erin was the reason I'd made it home ALIVE! Just the thought of seeing her face and talking to her again made me smile.

I planned to join the computer club like she'd suggested. Then we'd hang out together after school, play video games, and become good friends.

UNLESS!! YIKES! I couldn't even think about it!

I got a really sick feeling in the pit of my stomach.

WHAT if Erin's parents had found out that she'd SNUCK out of the house in the middle of the night (to help ME!) and . . .

ERIN

. . . SHIPPED HER OFF TO MILITARY SCHOOL?!

It would be all MY fault!

I would have TOTALLY RUINED both of our lives!

And I'd NEVER forgive myself for that!

The bus finally arrived at South Ridge Middle School and came to a screeching halt.

Kids piled into the aisle, still chatting excitedly about their three-day weekends.

I took a deep breath, stood up, and trudged off the bus.

16. TESTING! IS THIS THING ON?!

I barely recognized South Ridge Middle School! Police officers were everywhere. There was crime-scene tape blocking off all the entrances into the school, with cops standing guard.

Teachers and students were crowded outside the main door. Everyone looked a little freaked out!!

I scanned the crowd for Erin, but I didn't see her.

"Do you know what happened?" some kid asked another.

I moved in closer to hear the word on the street.

"I heard the chemistry lab accidentally exploded and destroyed the entire school!"

"My brother said some high school kids vandalized the building as their senior prank!"

"My BFF said they found a dead body in a locker!"

YIKES! That last rumor could have been TRUE if
I hadn't escaped from MY locker! . . .

MY FINAL MESSAGE TO THE WORLD!

"My sister said the school is going to be shut down for the rest of the year!" said a girl who was wearing WAY too much lip gloss. "So I'm going to transfer to Westchester Country Day! All my BFFs go there!"

The rumors were WILD!

Finally Principal Smith came out of the building with a bullhorn, and the huge crowd quieted down.

But when he tried to talk, his bullhorn emitted an earsplitting squeal. Everyone shuddered and covered their ears.

It was almost as shrill as Megan's screaming after she discovered I'd used up all her bubble bath! (Hey, I'd been stuck in that filthy Dumpster FOREVER! It wasn't MY fault I needed to take a warm, relaxing bubble bath for FOUR consecutive nights before I FINALLY felt totally CLEAN!)

The principal valiantly addressed his students and teachers as we anxiously clung to his every word! . . .

MY PRINCIPAL, MAKING AN ANNOUNCEMENT

"Good morning, South Ridge Middle School students and staff! Thank you for your patience. I'm happy to announce that our school will be OPEN today and classes will resume as scheduled!"

Most everyone groaned. A few kids clapped excitedly.

"I just have a few announcements before we enter our hallowed halls," Principal Smith continued.

It was getting hard to breathe. I dug through my backpack for my inhaler and took the last dose.

JUST GREAT! I sent my mom a text letting her know I was out of medicine while the principal gave us details about the break-in over the weekend.

He then explained that some classrooms would be off-limits during the police investigation, like the computer lab and the biology room, but that signs would be posted instructing us where to go instead.

While he was talking, I FINALLY spotted Erin in the crowd, but she didn't see me.

I breathed a HUGE sigh of relief!

At least her parents HADN'T shipped her off to a military school! YET, anyway!

"One last thing!" Principal Smith continued. "I do not want any of you or your parents to worry about the safety of South Ridge Middle School. We have a state-of-the-art surveillance system, and I'll be reviewing the footage with the investigation team after lunch today. But, most important, we'll soon have a private security team in place to ensure YOUR safety during school hours. We WILL get to the bottom of this break-in and APPREHEND the individuals involved! You have MY word on that!"

The crowd cheered!

Then the principal removed the police tape blocking the main door and instructed us to report to our first-hour classes.

Students and staff were slowly herded into the school.

Erin finally saw me, and our eyes locked.

Then we desperately pushed our way through the massive crowd to get to each other.

It was kind of like one of those cheesy teen romance movies that my sister is obsessed with. Only, in the movie the perfect couple walks hand in hand to their lockers and then to a happily ever after!

WHO was I kidding?!

If the police reviewed the school's surveillance footage and saw me on there, it was . . .

GAME OVER!

I'd get suspended and end up homeschooled by my grandma.

After what seemed like forever, Erin and I were finally standing face-to-face. We were thinking the EXACT same thing! . . .

We were BOTH FREAKING OUT! And the LAST thing we
wanted was to end up in even WORSE trouble!

17. THEFT, THREATS, AND THUG-GERY

Erin and I barely had a chance to talk. Teachers were stationed in the halls to keep the students moving, and we were quickly herded into our first-hour classrooms.

"Max! I'll see you in science! We'll talk then!" Erin shouted, and waved as she disappeared into a throng of students filing into honors English.

I felt a lot better knowing she was okay.

We'd be able to talk more freely in second-hour science and figure out what we should do.

You know, to lessen the possibility of me getting either suspended or arrested by lunchtime.

Just the thought of going to my first-hour class made me feel nauseated.

I seriously thought about hanging out in the library or hiding in the boys' bathroom.

But that would mean yet another unexcused absence, and I was already in enough trouble.

I trudged into my math class and shuddered at the sight of Thug.

He just stared at me with this huge smirk.

I wanted to KNOCK that smirk right off his face! With a CHAIR!! But I didn't.

I knew he was probably wondering how I'd finally escaped from my locker after he'd thrown me in there Friday after school.

"Did you have a nice weekend, BARF?!" he laughed.

Things quickly went from bad to worse! My teacher told me to take a seat in the back of the room to make up a POP QUIZ I'd missed last Wednesday.

Thanks to Thug, I'd been trapped inside my locker during first hour on THAT day too! . . .

ME, TRYING TO TAKE A QUIZ WHILE
THUG ACTS LIKE A FOUR-YEAR-OLD!

I was having a hard enough time with the quiz! And now I had to deal with Thug's slimy SPITBALLS?!!

It seemed like the guy HATED me!

Or maybe he was jealous that Erin and I were friends.

I had to admit, it was VERY obvious he was CRUSHING on her!

This is what happened last week. . . .

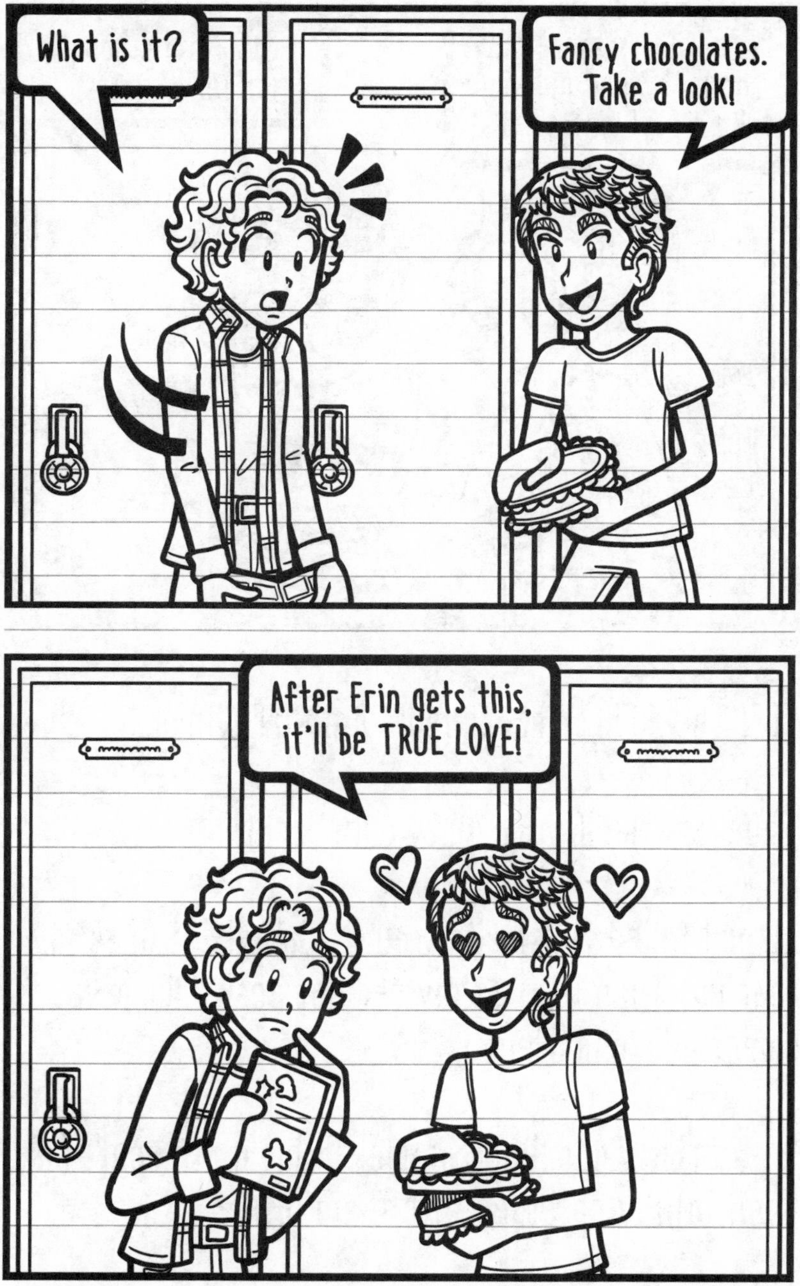
What is it?
Fancy chocolates. Take a look!
After Erin gets this, it'll be TRUE LOVE!

YES! This REALLY happened! I am NOT lying.

Thug has the IQ of a dirty gym sock!

After I ~~failed~~ finished my quiz, I handed it in to my teacher. Then I sat at my regular desk, which was directly behind Thug.

He was busy doodling zombies in his math book. He's been totally obsessed with them lately.

Thug says a zombie apocalypse could ac~~~
happen and DESTROY mankind! But zom~~~
BRAINS. So Thug was SAFE.

I pulled my math textbook out of my backpack. And when I opened my book, something fell out and slid into the aisle several feet in front of me.

YIKES! IT WAS MY DAD'S SUPER-VALUABLE, RARE COMIC BOOK!!

I'd totally forgotten I had shoved it inside my math book on Saturday morning to HIDE it from my dad!!

I reached into the aisle and quickly grabbed it!

WHEW!! CLOSE CALL! I'd almost DIED trying to get that thing back from those burglars!

I was about to put it away when . . . **SNATCH!!**

The comic literally DISAPPEARED right before my eyes! I stared at my empty hand in SHOCK!!

THUG, SNATCHING MY COMIC BOOK!!

I finally grabbed on to my comic book. But HE wouldn't let go.

"THUG!! WHAT are you doing?" I hissed.

"WHAT does it look like?" he snarled. "I want it!"

I pulled the book hard. He pulled back even harder!

We were having a ~~TUG-OF-WAR~~ THUG-OF-WAR with my DAD'S comic book!

And NO! I DIDN'T have PERMISSION to bring it to school the FIRST time or the SECOND time!

"Give it back! It's MINE!" I said under my breath.

"Not anymore!" Thug said. "It's MINT condition!"

But it wouldn't be for long with us fighting over it! I broke into a cold sweat.

OH, CRUD! THUG WAS GOING TO RIP MY DAD'S COMIC BOOK IN HALF!!

So I let go of it before he damaged it.

"Thanks! YOU LOSER!" Thug smirked as the bell rang, signaling the end of class.

Calling me a LOSER was an understatement! I was hopelessly TRAPPED in a LOSE-LOSE scenario.

If I hadn't let go of the book, Thug would have ripped it to shreds trying to take it from me. And if I reported Thug for STEALING IT, the school was going to contact my parents. The LAST thing I needed right then was more DRAMA at school!

Thug shoved the comic book into his backpack, grinned at me, and walked out of the classroom.

I was SO upset, my panic attack was having a panic attack!

I HATE the way Thug makes me hate MYSELF! He is a huge POOP STAIN on the UNDERWEAR of HUMANITY! For REAL!

18. SPILLING MY GUTS CAN BE MESSY!

I was a NERVOUS WRECK by the time I got to my physical science class.

Principal Smith was going to view the school's surveillance video today after lunch. And if he saw ME, my life was pretty much OVER!

My parents were going to snatch me out of this school so fast, it would make my head spin.

Then I'd be stuck getting HOMESCHOOLED by my grandma FOREVER! Well, at least until I graduated from ~~high school~~ COLLEGE!

To make matters worse, Thug had just STOLEN my DAD'S comic book!

That meant I'd ALSO be GROUNDED until I graduated from ~~high school~~ COLLEGE!

My life STANK worse than the two-week-old mystery meat rotting in the Dumpster behind the school!

I couldn't help but overhear two students sitting nearby talking about the classroom that was blocked off by crime-scene tape.

They said one of the class pets—a giant python named Tinkerbell—had escaped from a bio classroom in the chaos over the weekend and was missing!

But a janitor had found her asleep on a shelf in the library thirty minutes ago. Thank goodness!

Tinkerbell had helped me take down Ralph, the ringleader of the thieves! In my eyes, she was a ten-foot-long slithering SUPERHERO! . . .

TINKERBELL, THE S-S-SUPERHERO!

"Hi, Max!" Erin smiled as she took the lab stool next to me. "Finally we can talk. So, I guess you made it home safely!"

"Yeah, I did! What about you?"

"Same here! My parents didn't even know I'd snuck out!" she whispered. "And they even said that I'll get my computer back on Friday!"

"That's good news!" I said, relieved. At least we'd be able to communicate with each other again after school hours.

Then I told her the bad news about my comic book getting stolen AGAIN! This time by THUG!

Suddenly I felt HOPELESS and completely overwhelmed by a sense of impending DOOM!

It was my very cruddy DESTINY!

By the end of the day I was going to be FRONT-PAGE NEWS! . . .

MY MUG SHOT MAKES THE FRONT PAGE!

"Listen, Erin, I'm seriously thinking about confessing to Principal Smith! I really want to get this over with. The suspense of not knowing what's going to happen is driving me CRAZY!"

"Just try not to panic. It's going to be okay, Max!"

"No, it's NOT! When Smith sees me TRASHING the school in that surveillance video, I'm DEAD MEAT! I'll get suspended for sure!"

"The school got trashed because you were trying to STOP those THIEVES! And if YOU get suspended, I'LL get suspended too!" Erin said stubbornly. "We're in this TOGETHER!"

"I was afraid that you'd go down with me too, Erin. But YOU won't be on that video! And I'll NEVER tell anyone you helped me! I PROMISE!"

Erin is the smartest kid at our school! She loves science so much, she is ALSO taking honors bio! If she got into trouble, it could end up on her permanent record and impact her ability to attend college.

Erin has a bright future and is probably going to do AMAZING things! Like be president AND cure cancer AND figure out why banana-flavored candies never taste anything like bananas! . . .

ERIN'S CUTTING-EDGE RESEARCH ON BANANA-FLAVORED CANDIES!

The only thing WORSE than spending the rest of my life being homeschooled by my grandma would be knowing I had totally RUINED Erin's FUTURE!!

Suddenly my final decision was crystal clear! I knew exactly what I had to do. After class was over, I was going straight to Principal Smith and SPILLING MY GUTS!

About EVERYTHING!

Thug, my locker, the comic book, the burglars, sneaking into my house, the stuff I'd left on Mr. Howell's lawn, and the two cops.

Well, everything . . . except ERIN!

Then I'd clean out my locker and call my parents to come pick me up. Today was officially my LAST DAY at South Ridge Middle School!

Why did I ever think a TOTAL LOSER like ME would fit in at this place?!

Right then I was feeling just . . . AWFUL!

It was GAME OVER!

This time for REAL.

19. IT'S A HORRIBLE IDEA! SO LET'S DO IT!

I was really lucky to have Erin as a friend.

It was too bad I wasn't going to be around to get to know her better.

Of course, she tried to talk me out of my decision to confess to Principal Smith and leave South Ridge.

But I wouldn't listen. My mind was made up. It was time for me to accept responsibility for my actions!

And, most important, it was the only way I could avoid dragging Erin into this MESS.

"I just wish I knew what was on that video!" I muttered aloud. "Otherwise, staying at this school is way TOO risky!"

Erin just stared at me. Then, slowly, an evil grin spread across her face. . . .

IF YOU REALLY WANT TO ... HAT VIDEO, THEN LET'S ... O TAKE A LOOK AT IT!

... RAZY?!!

... NCED ERIN'S LOST HER MIND!

... member! This was YOUR idea! Not MINE!" She smirked.

MY IDEA?! NO! This was NOT MY IDEA!

As much as I liked Erin, I was not going to let her throw ME under the BUS! . . .

> NO WAY, ERIN! I AM NOT HELPING YOU HACK INTO SECURITY VIDEOS! I'M ALREADY IN ENOUGH TROUBLE! AND WHAT IF WE GET CAUGHT?! IT'S A HORRIBLE IDEA! BUT IT MIGHT WORK! SO LET'S DO IT!

ME, TELLING ERIN WHAT I THINK OF HER STUPID IDEA RIGHT TO HER FACE!

"I KNOW this will WORK, Max! So here's the plan. I'll hack into the surveillance video and take a quick look. If you're on there, you can confess as planned. But if you're NOT, you have nothing to worry about. Just CHILLAX! Either way, you'll come out ahead because you'll have the facts!"

Erin's plan was BRILLIANT! If I wasn't on the video, I'd just keep my big mouth shut!

PROBLEM SOLVED!! Then I'd get to stay at South Ridge ~~and hang out with Erin the rest of the school year!~~ SWEET!

SORRY about that, GRANDMA!!

All we needed was a COMPUTER. It had to be:

1. hooked into the school's security system

2. available for us to use

3. in a location where we wouldn't be seen by teachers, staff, students, or the authorities.

It seemed IMPOSSIBLE!

But after fifteen minutes of intense brainstorming, we came up with only ONE computer in the ENTIRE building that might possibly work!

I broke into a cold sweat just thinking about it.

Erin and I skipped lunch. Instead, we snuck up to the third floor.

Then we tiptoed down the hall until we saw the door of the classroom.

Yes! That dreaded BIO classroom!

The place where ~~Tinkerbell and~~ I had taken out RALPH!

Only now all the animals had been temporarily moved to a chemistry classroom on the first floor.

There was a janitor's cart outside it, but no janitor. Or anyone else, for that matter. . . .

ERIN AND ME, CASING THE BIO ROOM

The crime-scene tape had been removed from the door and lay nearby in a huge pile.

It was eerily quiet. My heart was pounding as I held my breath and turned the door handle.

20. MASTERS OF MISCHIEF!

To my surprise, the classroom door clicked open. Erin and I cautiously walked inside.

The room was a bigger mess than I'd remembered, and Erin's mouth dropped open in shock.

"Yeah, it got kind of crazy in here!" I muttered.

Textbooks and papers were scattered all over, and the "Beware" sign from Tinkerbell's aquarium was still lying on the floor. Chairs were toppled over, glass from broken beakers and test tubes littered the room, and a miniature rocket was stuck in the rib cage of a life-size plastic skeleton (don't ask, it's a long story)!

"Come on, let's do this so we can get out of here!" Erin said as she sat down at the teacher's desk.

I watched over her shoulder as she furiously typed on the keyboard. . . .

ERIN, HACKING INTO
THE SECURITY SYSTEM!

"YAY ME!" she finally whispered.

"Did you get in?" I asked.

"YES! I'M IN!" she said. "And since I'm probably breaking twenty-seven school rules and eleven laws, could you keep watch at the door and warn me if you see anyone?"

"SURE, ERIN! I'M ON IT!!"

I opened the door and peeked out into the empty hall. "It's all good! Most everyone is still at lunch."

I couldn't help but notice that Erin looked like a totally normal middle school student. She could have been checking her e-mail, posting on social media, watching YouTube, or doing her homework.

But my friend was actually hacking into the school's security system to view surveillance files, even before the authorities had seen them. And she was doing it all to help ME!

"DONE!" Erin said after about five minutes.

"So . . . um, WHAT did you see?" I asked hesitantly.

She sighed and stared at the floor. Then she bit her lip and blinked back tears.

I could tell it was really BAD news before she even answered.

"I'm really SORRY, Max! But based on what I just saw, it unfortunately looks like . . . WE'RE BOTH GOING TO BE STUCK HERE AT SOUTH RIDGE MIDDLE SCHOOL FOR THE REST OF THE YEAR!" she exclaimed happily.

It took a minute for everything to finally soak into my brain. "So you're saying I'm NOT in any of the surveillance footage?!" I asked excitedly.

"NOPE!! Most of it was those three CROOKS moving computers out of the lab into a hall near the exit door. They were yelling at each other and acting so goofy, it was like watching a reality TV show or something. But the weirdest part was when that pizza delivery guy showed up! Did those CLOWNS actually order a PIZZA while they were burglarizing our school?! Like, WHO does that?!"

I was so happy and relieved, I did my VICTORY DANCE inside my head! GO, MAX! GO, MAX!

"Erin, you had me totally FOOLED with the tears and all! You're REALLY a good actress!" I gushed.

"I'm even BETTER onstage! Dude, my Ice Princess will give you CHILLS!" she joked.

NO DOUBT! Erin is good at EVERYTHING! And her computer SKILLZ are SICK!!

"I need to put a copy of this on a thumb drive for safekeeping!" she said, digging around in her backpack. "What did I do with that thing?!"

I reached into my pocket and handed her my Masked Eagle of Doom superhero thumb drive.

"Now, that's CUTE!" she teased.

"It's actually . . . my little brother's!" I lied.
"I'm just borrowing it. For, um . . . a class project."

"But it's NOT as CUTE as THIS!" She whipped out a hot-pink glittery Princess Sugar Plum thumb drive from a pocket in her backpack. . . .

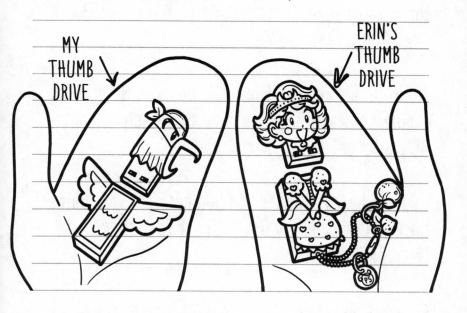

MY THUMB DRIVE

ERIN'S THUMB DRIVE

ERIN AND ME, COMPARING THUMB DRIVES

"YOURS definitely wins for cuteness!" I laughed.

After another minute Erin said, "Finished!"

She placed her thumb drive in her backpack. Then she handed mine back to me.

"PLEASE don't lose Eagle of Doom! Your little brother would never get over it!" She winked.

Then Erin stood up, cracked her knuckles, and shook out her hands like she'd just finished SLAYING a DRAGON or something.

"I got in, viewed the file, and copied it. No one should know you were here or that I helped you! NOW let's get out of here!"

I was so happy, I wanted to hug her. Can you blame me? She'd saved my life at least four times just this week!

Although we'd been through a lot together, I didn't think we were quite at the hugging stage yet.

So instead, I held up my hand for a high five.

"AWESOME WORK, ERIN!"

"Hey, you're the one who took down three criminals!" She smiled.

"But I couldn't have done it without YOU!" I said.

YES! Erin and I made an UNSTOPPABLE team!

We were the . . .

MASTERS OF MISCHIEF!

I glanced at my watch. "If we hurry, we still have time to make it back to the cafeteria for lunch!"

I grabbed the door handle to leave, when we suddenly heard footsteps, and then voices!

Erin and I FROZE!

Several men were standing right outside the door having a conversation.

We exchanged panicked glances and tried not to have a COMPLETE MELTDOWN! . . .

ERIN AND ME,
REALIZING WE WERE TRAPPED!!

That VOICE! It sounded VAGUELY familiar!

But I didn't have time to figure it out.

WE ONLY HAD SECONDS TO HIDE!

There was no way we'd make it to the storage closet on the other side of the room.

I looked around in sheer desperation.

Finally, I pointed, and Erin nodded in agreement.

It was a cruddy place to hide, but we didn't have much of a choice.

We scrambled into place just as the authorities entered the room!

21. A GAME OF ~~REVENGE~~ HIDE-AND-SEEK!

While I was hiding underneath that desk, I did a lot of serious thinking about my life.

Like how sometimes you REALLY want something to be real so you just ASSUME that it is.

Then later you're shocked to find out it's FAKE!

Well, that's what happened to my little brother when we were playing a board game last week. . . .

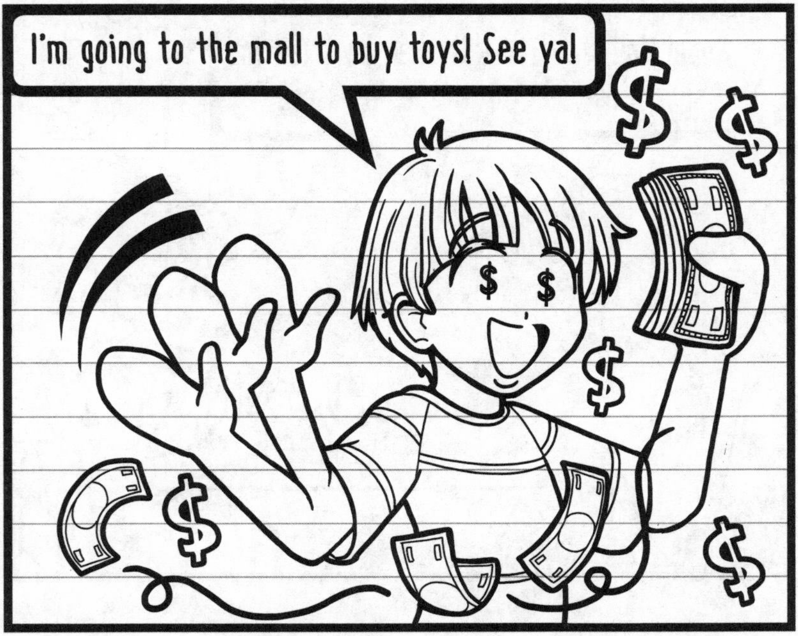
I'm going to the mall to buy toys! See ya!

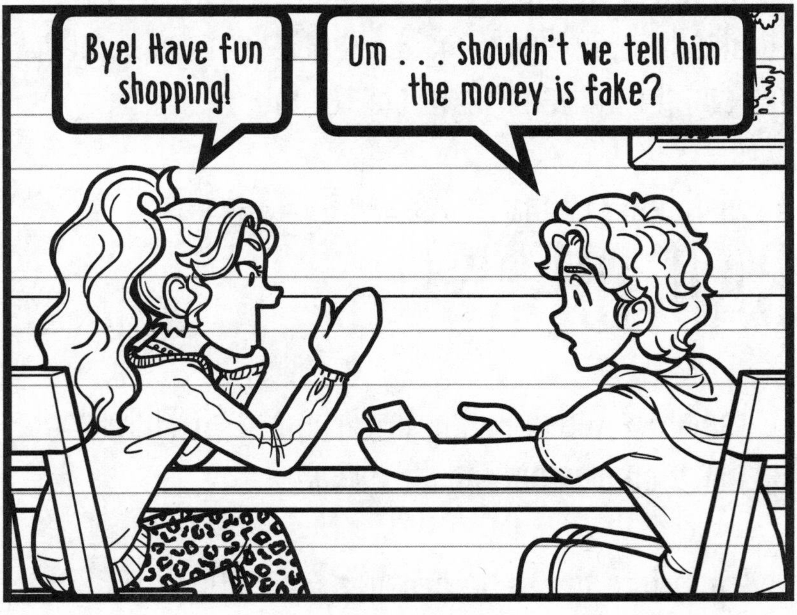
Bye! Have fun shopping!
Um . . . shouldn't we tell him the money is fake?

I'd Known it was RISKY to sneak into that bio room. I'd also Known there was a chance Erin and I could get caught and end up in big trouble.

My problem is that I have really fantastic . . .

BAD IDEAS!

So there we were! Hiding in a room with THREE security guards only inches away.

And just like my little brother's $50,000 . . .

... THOSE SECURITY GUARDS WERE
FAKER THAN MONOPOLY MONEY!!

There was only ONE thing WORSE than possibly getting caught hiding under that desk by the AUTHORITIES.

And it was possibly getting caught hiding under that desk by three RUTHLESS CRIMINALS!!

Erin and I could NOT believe this was actually happening to us!!

AGAIN!!!

We had no idea HOW those CREEPS had gotten into the school, WHY they were there, or WHAT they were doing!

But soon it all became VERY clear!!

"Hurry up, you MEATHEAD! Find that security footage and DELETE IT," Ralph growled. "Once the evidence is gone, they can't charge us with anything! Then our worries will be over!"

"Okay, boss! I'm working as fast as I can!" Tucker said. "WOW! LOOK AT THIS!"

"Is there a problem?! Are we too late?! If we're on that footage, we're JAILBIRDS!" Ralph sputtered. "WHAT'S WRONG?!"

"Nothing," Tucker answered. "I'm just surprised the new photo I uploaded this morning of my cat, Mr. Fuzzybottoms, has already gotten THREE likes! SEE? Can you believe it?!"

"Did you say LIKES?!" Ralph snarled. "How would you LIKE me to shove that keyboard down your throat? Quit wasting time, Tucker! According to the police scanner, they're going to be viewing this security footage after lunch! So get the lead out!"

"Speaking of lunch, I'm STARVING!" Moose whined. "There's a cafeteria here, right, boss? Maybe we can grab a BITE to EAT!"

"Sorry, Moose! YOU'RE not going to be able to BITE anything! If you don't SHUT your TRAP, I'm gonna knock your TEETH out! Every last one of 'em. Now both of you, try to FOCUS!"

"Good news, boss!" Tucker finally announced. "That password you lifted from the office Friday night actually worked. I just pulled up the security file for Friday. And . . . BAM!! I just DELETED it!"

The men high-fived each other!

"Now, that's what I'm talking about!" Ralph exclaimed. "Listen, gentlemen, to celebrate our success, how about a fancy meal at a swanky restaurant? After we leave here, I'm taking both of you to Crazy Burger! We'll eat like KINGS!"

"THANKS, BOSS!" Tucker and Moose grinned.

Ralph continued. "But first we have a really important meeting we need to get to. It's going to put us in the BIG LEAGUES! We're done with petty crime. I should have invested in these fake security guard uniforms years ago. Now let's get out of here."

Then they opened the door and disappeared. Erin and I just stayed right there under that desk. We were too STUNNED and too SCARED to move!

22. STRANGER DANGER!

It was hard to believe that Ralph, Moose, and Tucker were CRAZY enough to dress up like security guards, enter the school, and ERASE the surveillance footage.

Like, WHO does THAT?!!

The footage that showed them at the school stealing computers no longer existed.

Now the authorities would NEVER connect them to the crime, and there were no other witnesses.

Well, OKAY! No other witnesses except ME, ERIN, and PRINCESS SUGAR PLUM.

"Come on, Max! We need to go straight to Principal Smith and tell him everything that just happened!" Erin fumed as she crawled out from under the desk. "We can't just let these JERKS get away with this!"

"Erin, that's exactly what I wanted to do all along.

But YOU talked me out of it. At this point I really don't care if I get in trouble and end up being homeschooled by my grandma again. I don't want YOU to get in over YOUR head!" I explained. "You've got way more to lose than I do!"

Erin just stared at me. "Okay, Max! I get it. We shouldn't tell Smith anything that he could possibly use against us. What if I say that I went to the bio room to get my . . . um . . ." Erin looked around the room and spotted the plastic skeleton. "To get my ROCKET, and I overheard those guys talking!"

"Yeah, that might work! But how do we know they're not STILL hanging around?" I asked.

"Actually, we don't! But it seemed like they were in a big hurry to leave. And Ralph said they had an important meeting they needed to get to. Also, they planned to eat at Crazy Burger. That's THREE reasons why I think they're gone!"

Erin had a really good point!

"Okay! Let's go!" I finally agreed.

We hurried down the stairs to the main floor and then raced down the hall to the principal's office.

The principal's secretary was talking on the phone.

"Is Principal Smith in his office?" I interrupted. "We need to talk to him! It's really important!"

She covered the phone with one hand and looked super annoyed. "I'm sorry! He's in his office, but he's NOT available right now! I can schedule an appointment for you later this afternoon if you—I"

"THANKS!" Erin and I said as we rushed right past her and BARGED into the principal's office!

"PRINCIPAL SMITH!" Erin shouted frantically. "I'M REALLY SORRY TO INTERRUPT YOU! BUT WE RUSHED DOWN HERE TO LET YOU KNOW THAT I JUST SAW SOME SUSPICIOUS-LOOKING MEN INSIDE THE SCHOOL! I THINK THEY'RE DANGEROUS! SO PLEASE CALL THE POLICE IMMEDIATELY IF YOU SEE . . ."

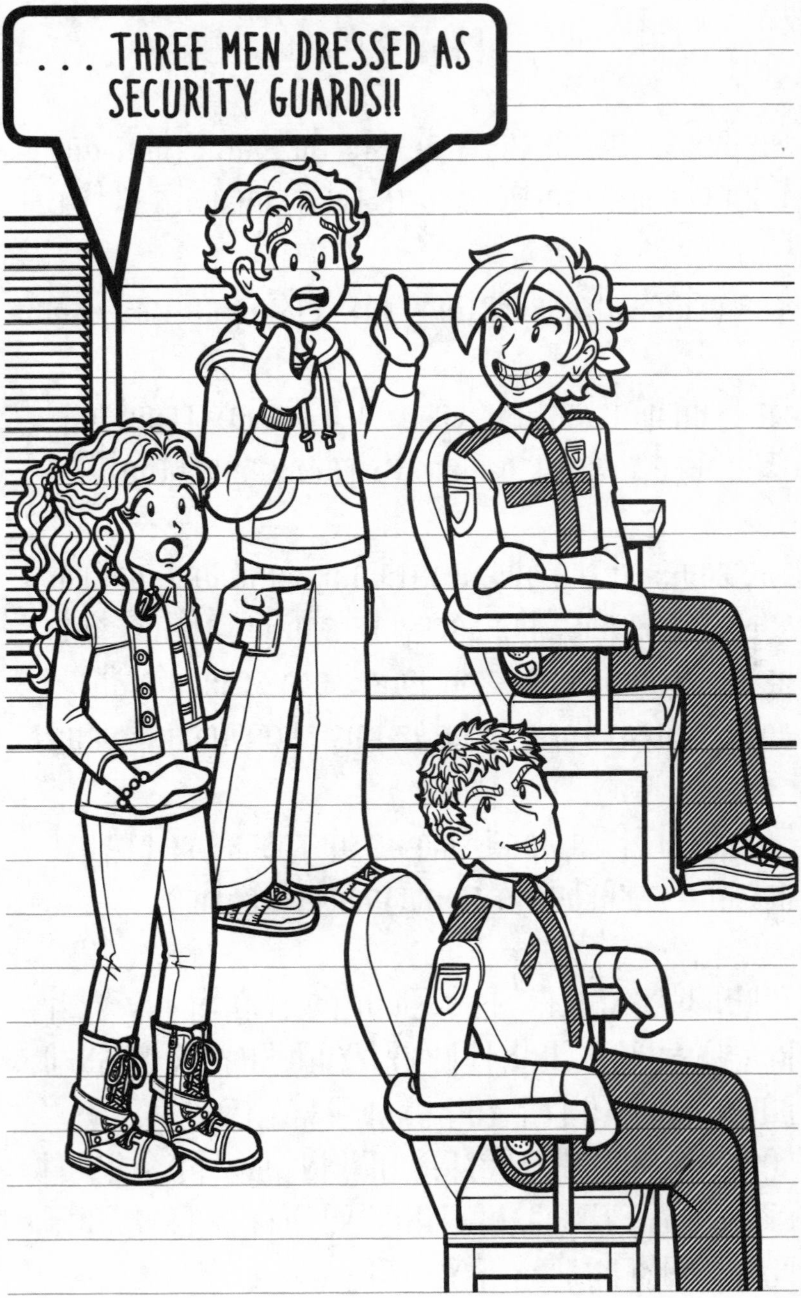
. . . THREE MEN DRESSED AS SECURITY GUARDS!!

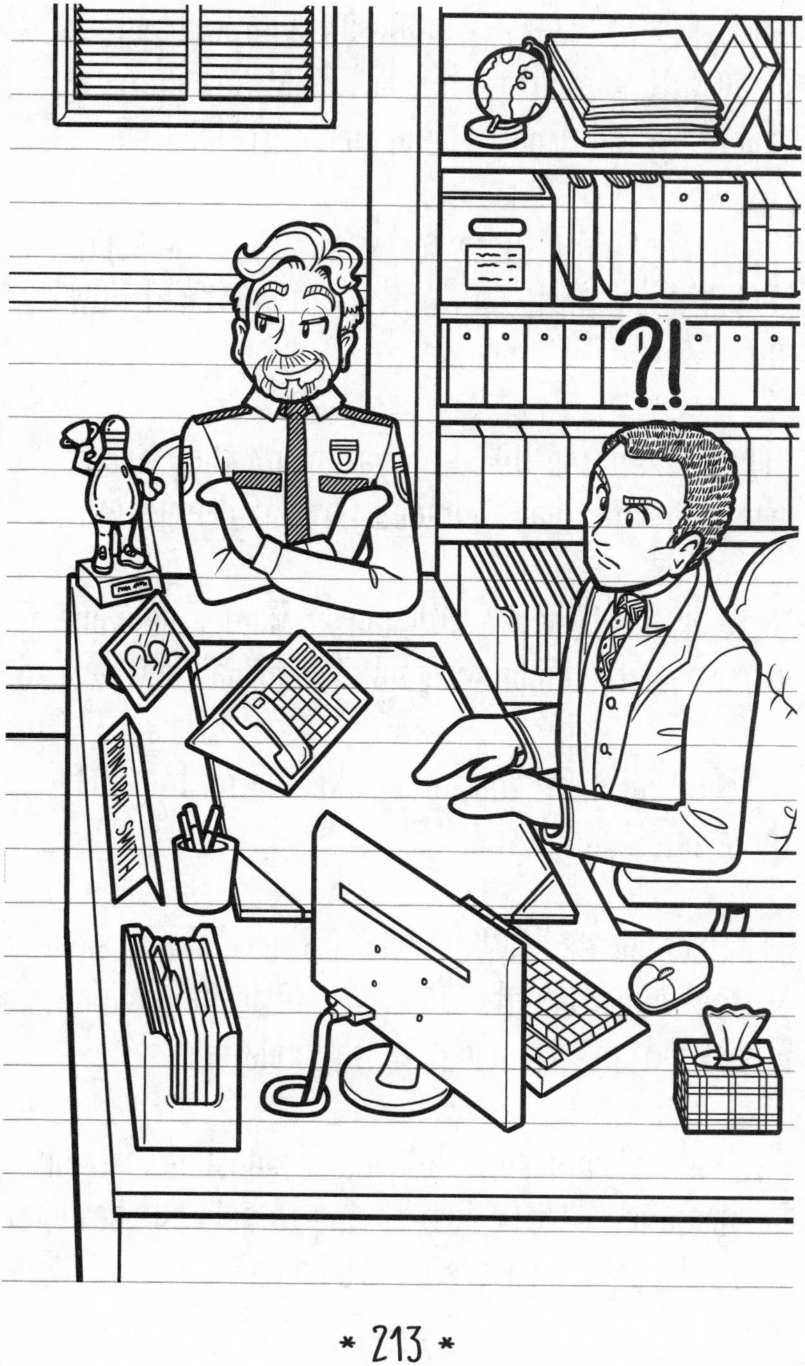
?!
PRINCIPAL SMITH

"MAX?! ERIN?! WHAT IS GOING ON?! I'd be happy to speak with you both later, but right now I'm in an important meeting!" the principal scolded.

"Principal Smith, we're sorry! But this is REALLY, REALLY important!! Can we talk to you right NOW?! Um . . . ALONE?!" I pleaded.

"These men are NOT who you think they are!" Erin said. "You have no idea why they're here!"

"Actually, I DO! They're with, um . . . what's the name of your security company again?" Principal Smith asked.

"STEEL SECURITY! You know, like the metal. NOT the crime!" Ralph smirked.

"They've agreed to VOLUNTEER their time to help protect our students and assist with the ongoing investigation." Principal Smith explained.

"We feel it's our civic duty as responsible citizens." Ralph smiled. "We're just trying to help out however we can! The YOUTH are our FUTURE!"

Principal Smith continued. "Due to our recent budgetary issues, I've been authorized to accept any donations of goods or services from the community to help us get past this unfortunate incident. These gentlemen have even agreed to provide twenty-four-hour security for our computer lab! We believe our new computers were being targeted."

"That's correct!" Ralph said. "We'll protect YOUR computers just like they were our OWN!"

I shuddered! Principal Smith had no idea he was dealing with three RUTHLESS CRIMINALS! And now the ENTIRE school was in DANGER! That's when Erin totally lost it! "Principal Smith, I was . . . backing up files for the computer club, and somehow I, um . . . accidentally downloaded a, um . . . SECURITY file. You really NEED to take a look at this!" she said as she placed her thumb drive on his desk. "RIGHT NOW!"

Ralph glared at Erin. "Well, I hope you didn't carelessly ERASE any of the security footage, young lady! We need to check that out RIGHT NOW!" he said as he grabbed Erin's thumb drive. . . .

RALPH, VOWING TO CATCH
THE SUSPECTS!

YES! Ralph actually accused Erin of carelessly ERASING a surveillance video file! After THEY'D erased it THEMSELVES in the bio classroom!

It was quite obvious that Ralph was a THIEF and a PATHOLOGICAL LIAR! I resisted the urge to give him a BEATDOWN right there in Principal Smith's office!

It pretty much went DOWNHILL from there.

Principal Smith threatened us with detentions for rudely interrupting his meeting and threw us out of his office!

He said he couldn't talk to us today because a team from the police department was arriving soon to view the security footage with him. So he had his secretary give us an appointment for tomorrow.

But tomorrow was going to be too late!

I already had a hunch how all of this was going to play out from reading my comic books and watching all those CSI crime shows on television.

Once they discovered that the school's security footage had been deleted, Erin was going to be blamed, thanks to Ralph.

But they'd ALSO want to see the security file SHE'D "accidentally downloaded to HER thumb drive while backing up material for the computer club."

At some point Principal Smith was going to ask Ralph for Erin's thumb drive because it possibly contained potential evidence.

Ralph desperately needed to know how much Erin knew. So he was going to view and then erase Erin's thumb drive as soon as possible! Like, BEFORE the police team arrived.

And he needed to do it at a computer where there would be no witnesses.

If my hunch was correct, any minute now those three crooks would be rushing out of that meeting and heading BACK to that computer in the bio classroom with Erin's thumb drive.

"I can't believe Ralph accused ME of erasing that file!" Erin sniffed, blinking back tears. "What are we going to do now, Max?!"

I was pretty sure Erin's tears were real this time. I couldn't help but feel really bad for her.

"I think those creeps are heading back to the bio computer to check your thumb drive and erase it. Only this time, we're going to take a video of them doing it! With my cell phone!" I fumed.

"SORRY! But I am NOT going to hide under that desk AGAIN!" Erin protested. "We were lucky they didn't see us the first time!"

"We're not going back INSIDE the room. That would be way too dangerous. We'll have a much better view from that VENT near the ceiling!"

"MAX, THAT'S CRAZY!" Erin exclaimed, wiping a tear that had rolled down her cheek. "Our situation is HOPELESS! How in the world are we going to get inside a vent in that room?!"

I nervously opened my locker. "Through here?!" . . .

OMG!

ME, SHOWING ERIN MY SECRET ENTRANCE
INTO THE VENTILATION SYSTEM!

I'd had quite enough of those three . . .

CLOWNS!

For the past five days, they'd pretty much turned my world upside down. Erin's, too! My ~~crush~~ friend was actually in tears.

Those CROOKS had STARTED this war. And now I was going to FINISH it.

Sorry, but Max C. was NOT going down without a FIGHT!

If they wanted a piece of me, it was . . .

GAME ON!

23. BOILER ROOM SMACKDOWN!

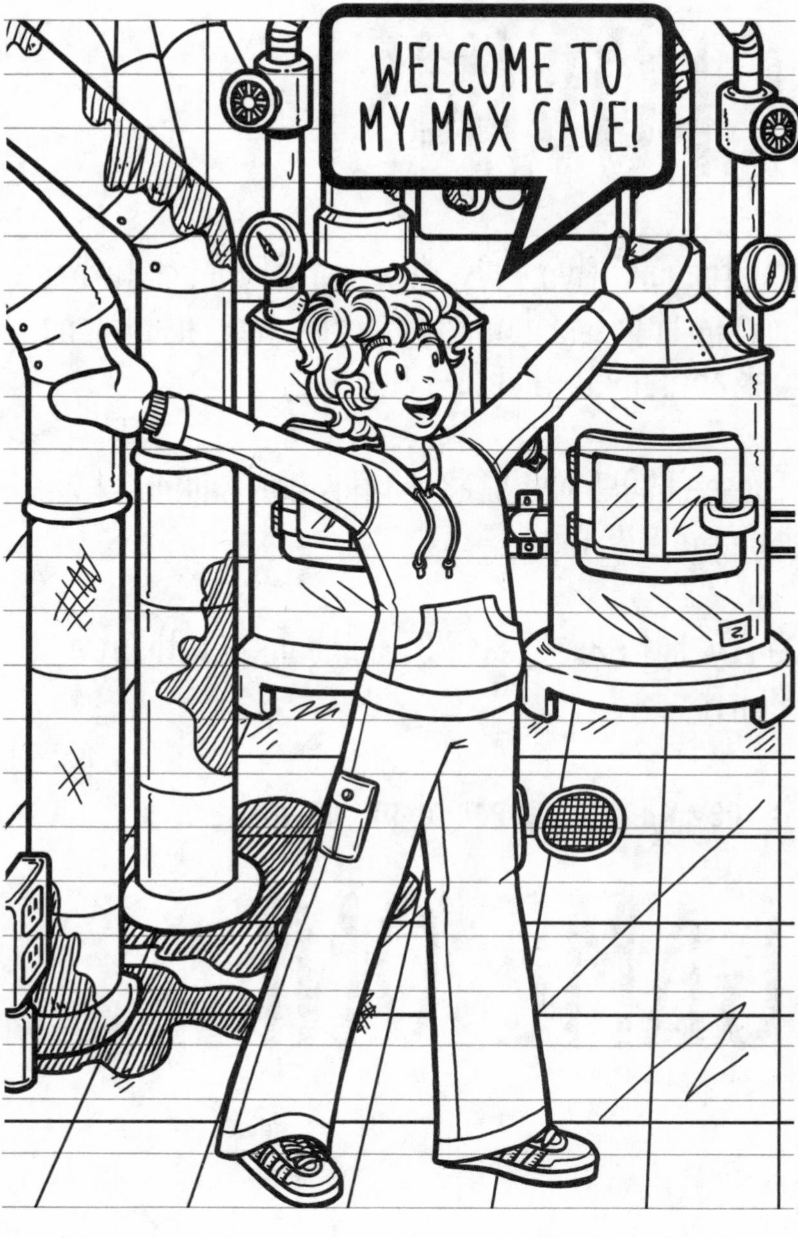
WELCOME TO
MY MAX CAVE!

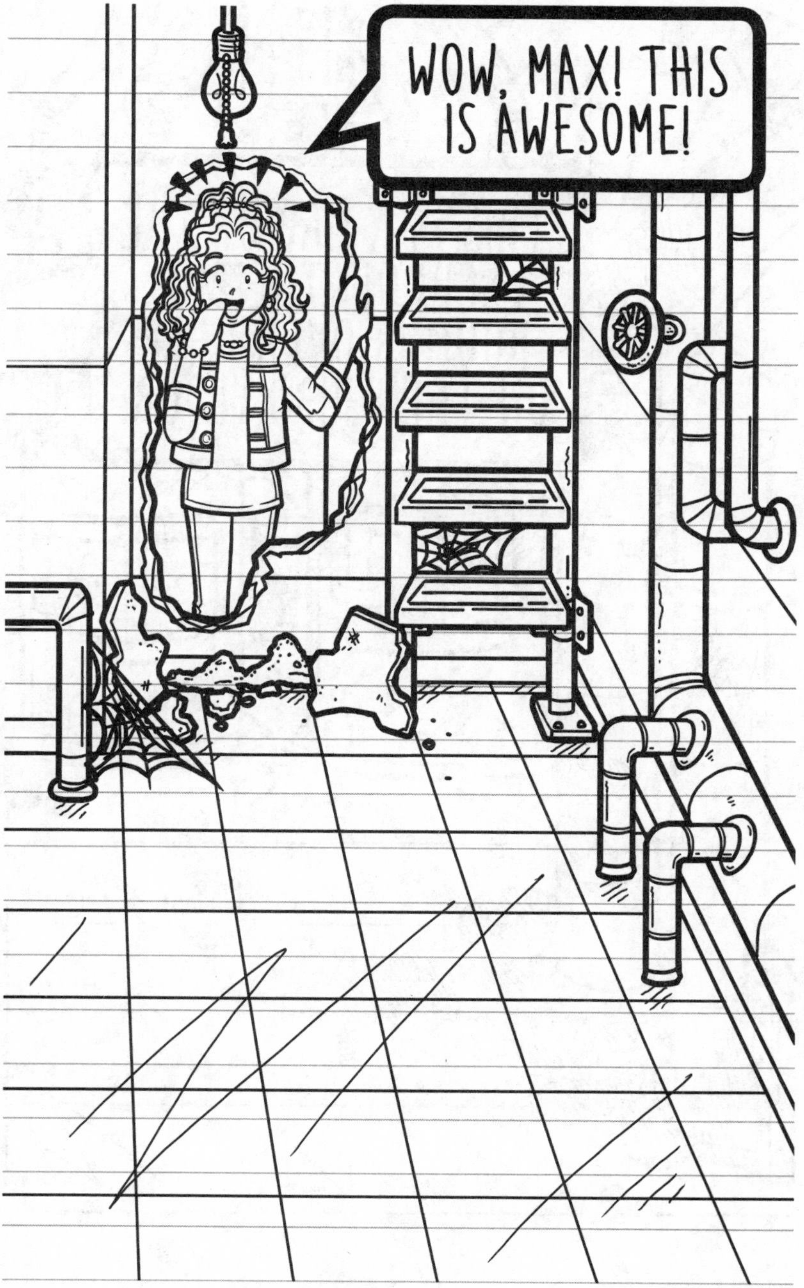
WOW, MAX! THIS IS AWESOME!

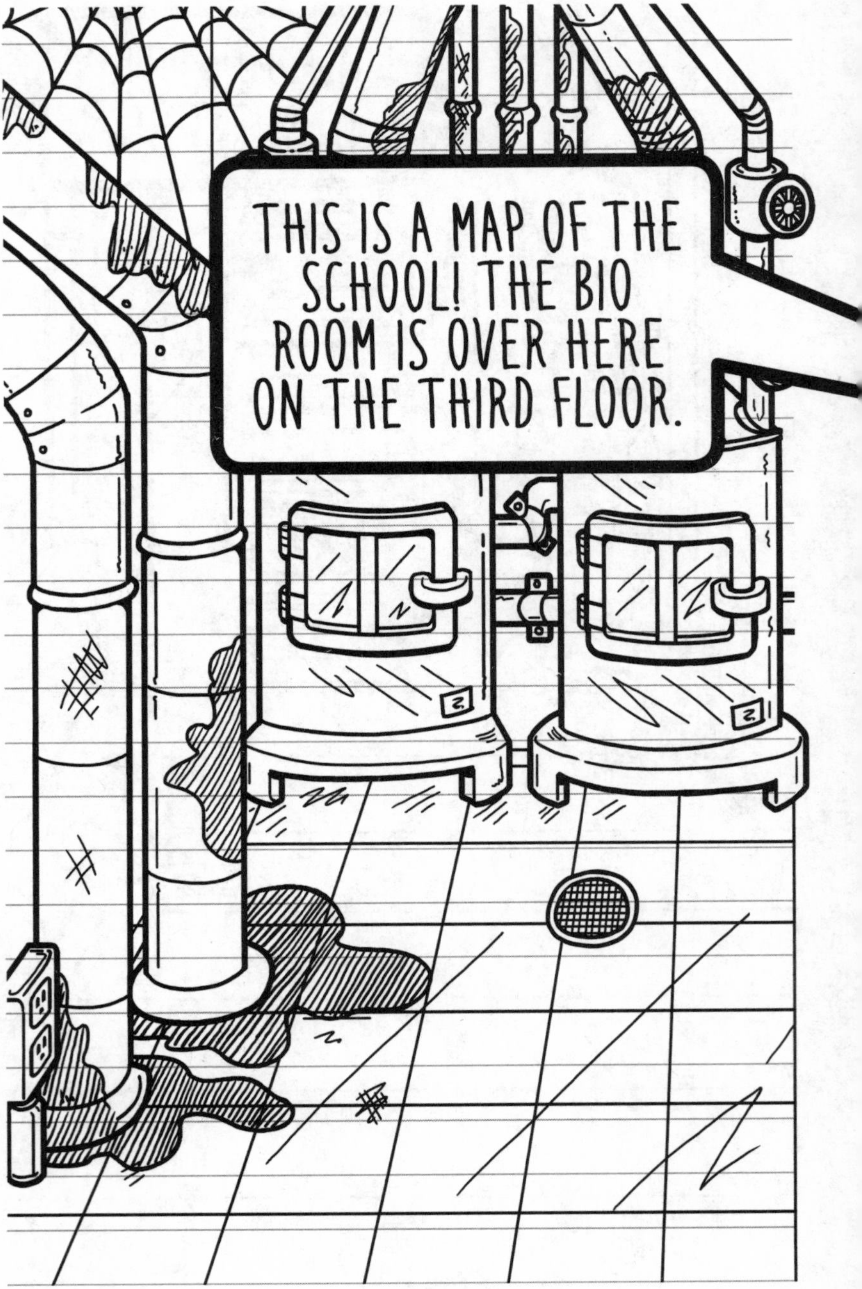
THIS IS A MAP OF THE SCHOOL! THE BIO ROOM IS OVER HERE ON THE THIRD FLOOR.

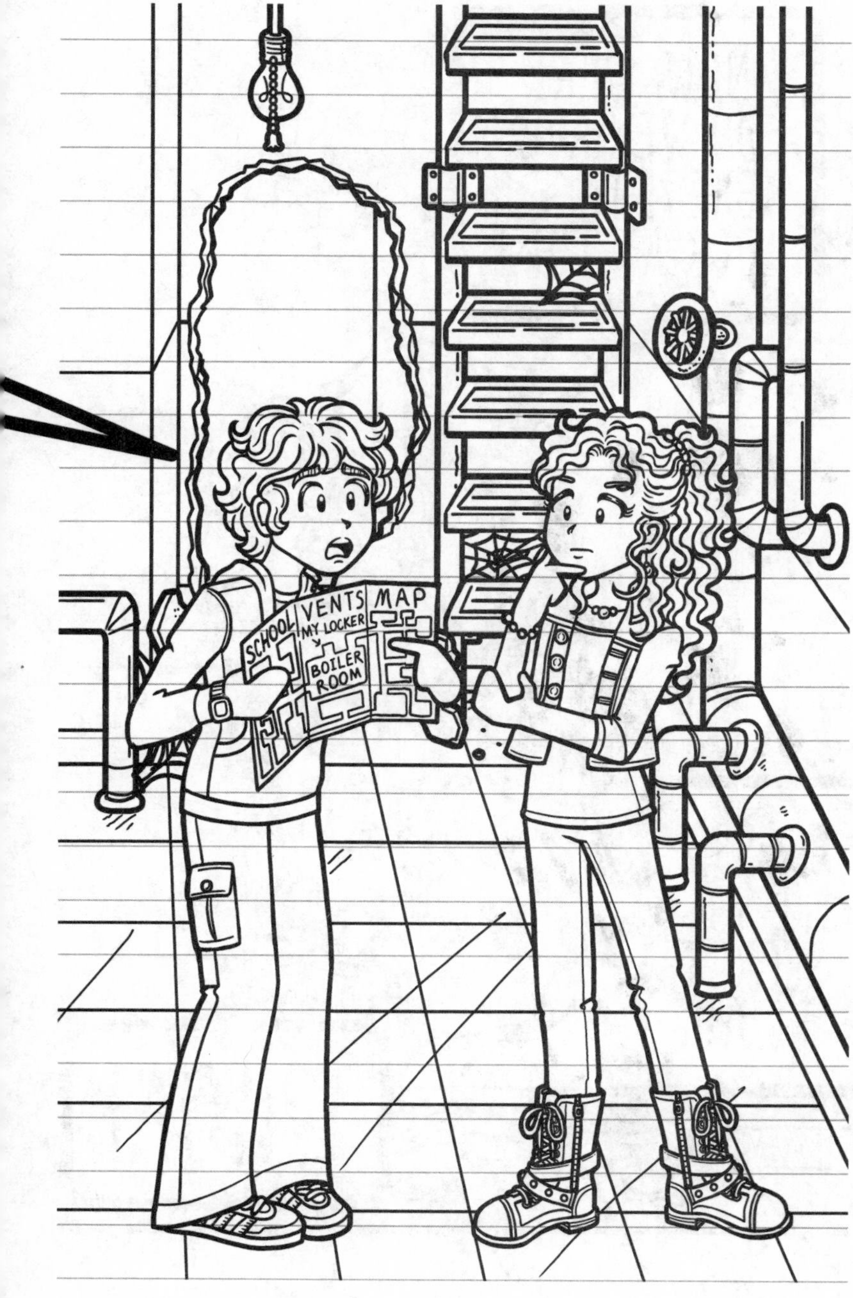
SCHOOL VENTS MAP
MY LOCKER
BOILER ROOM

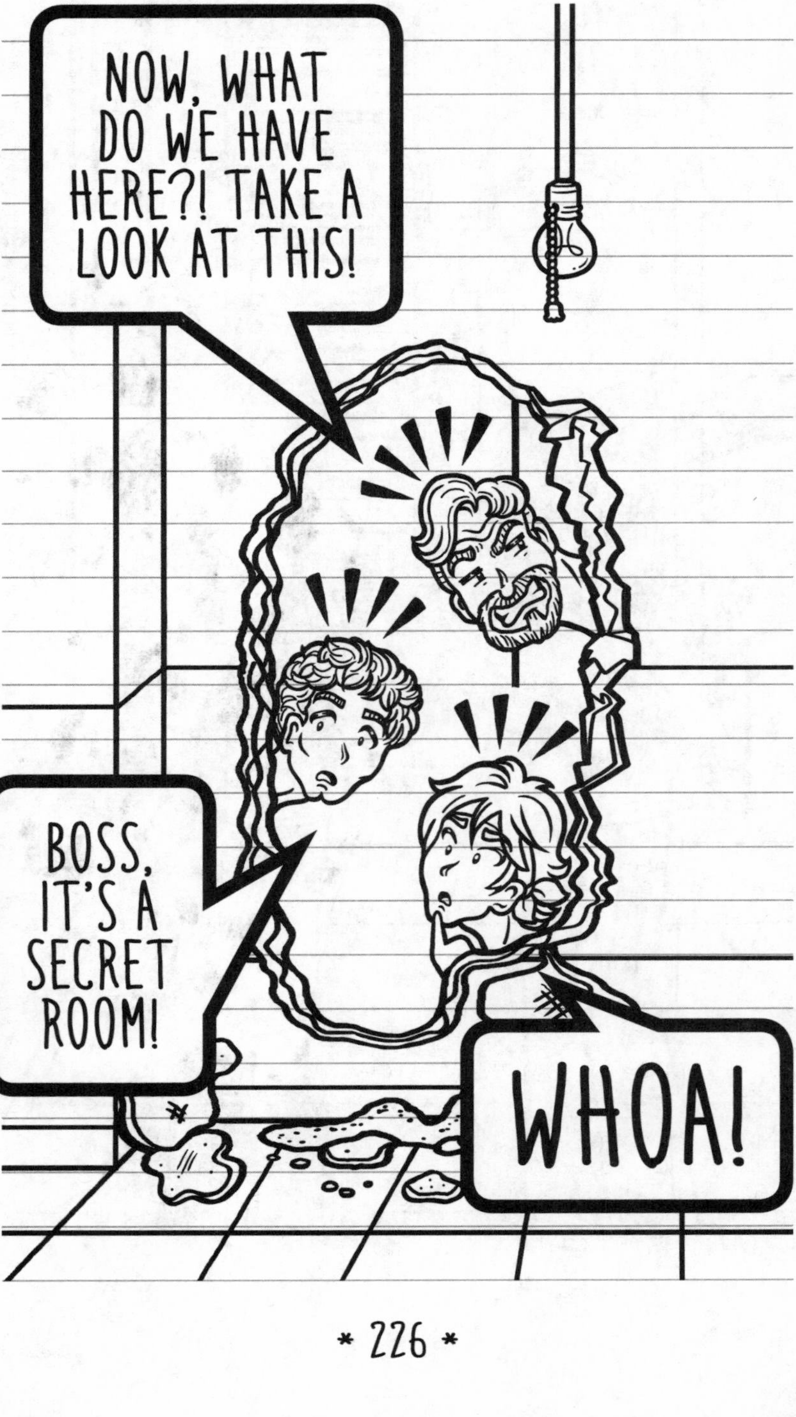
NOW, WHAT DO WE HAVE HERE?! TAKE A LOOK AT THIS!
BOSS, IT'S A SECRET ROOM!
WHOA!

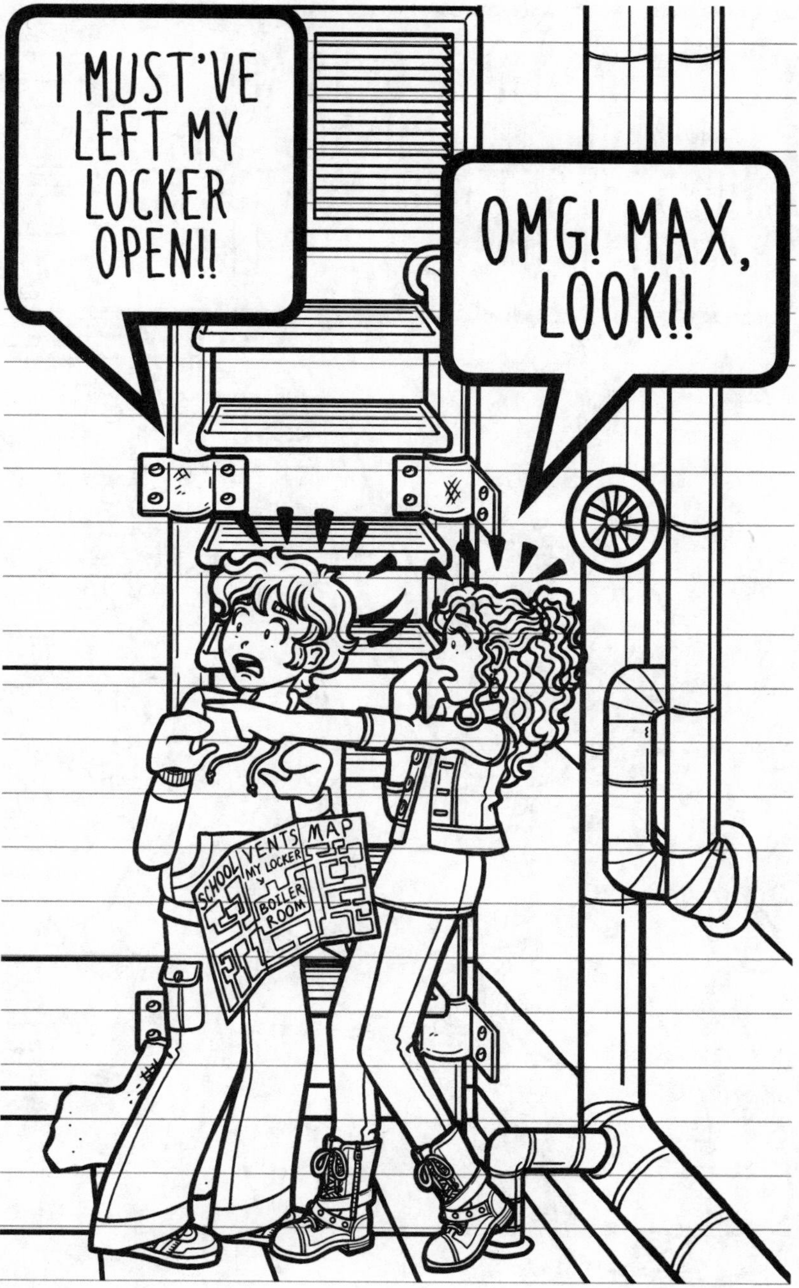
I MUST'VE LEFT MY LOCKER OPEN!!
OMG! MAX, LOOK!!
SCHOOL VENTS MAP
MY LOCKER
BOILER ROOM

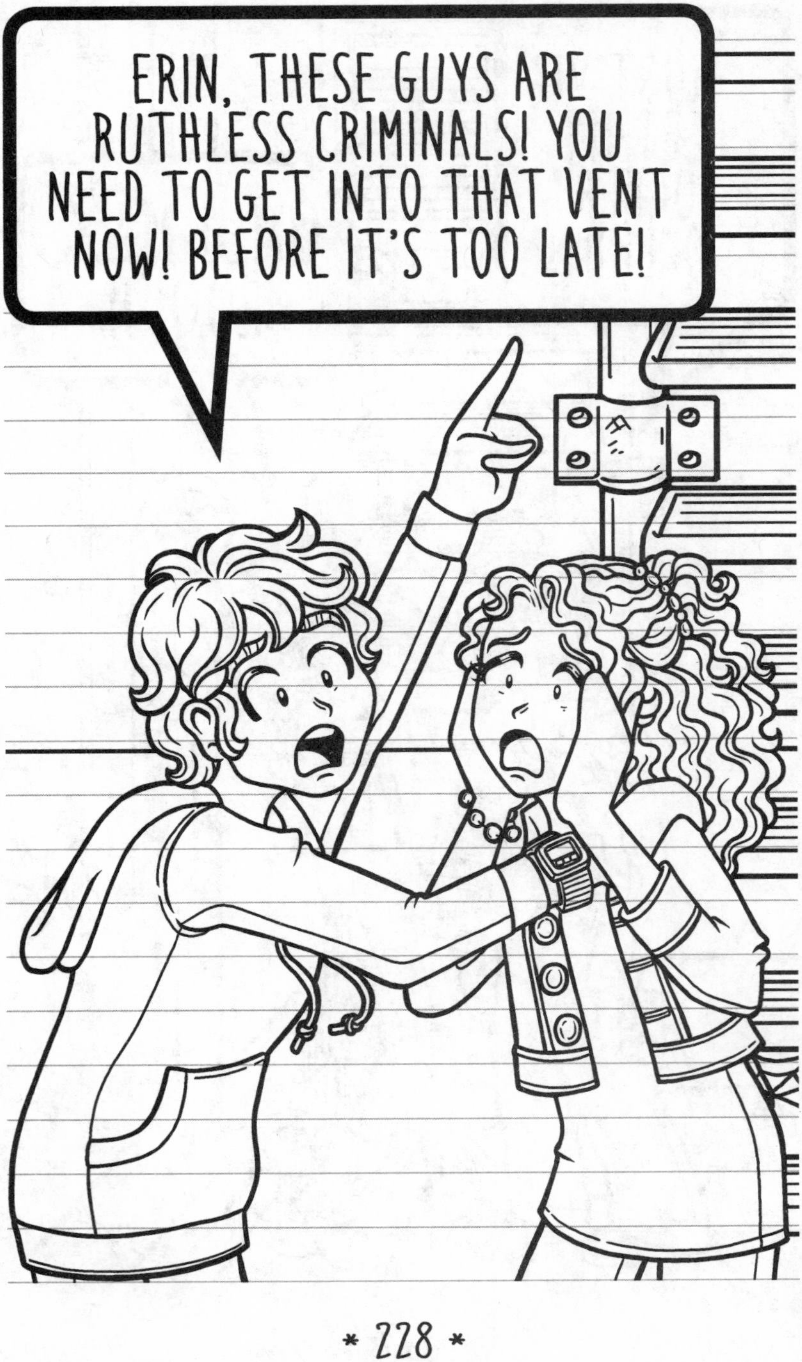
ERIN, THESE GUYS ARE RUTHLESS CRIMINALS! YOU NEED TO GET INTO THAT VENT NOW! BEFORE IT'S TOO LATE!

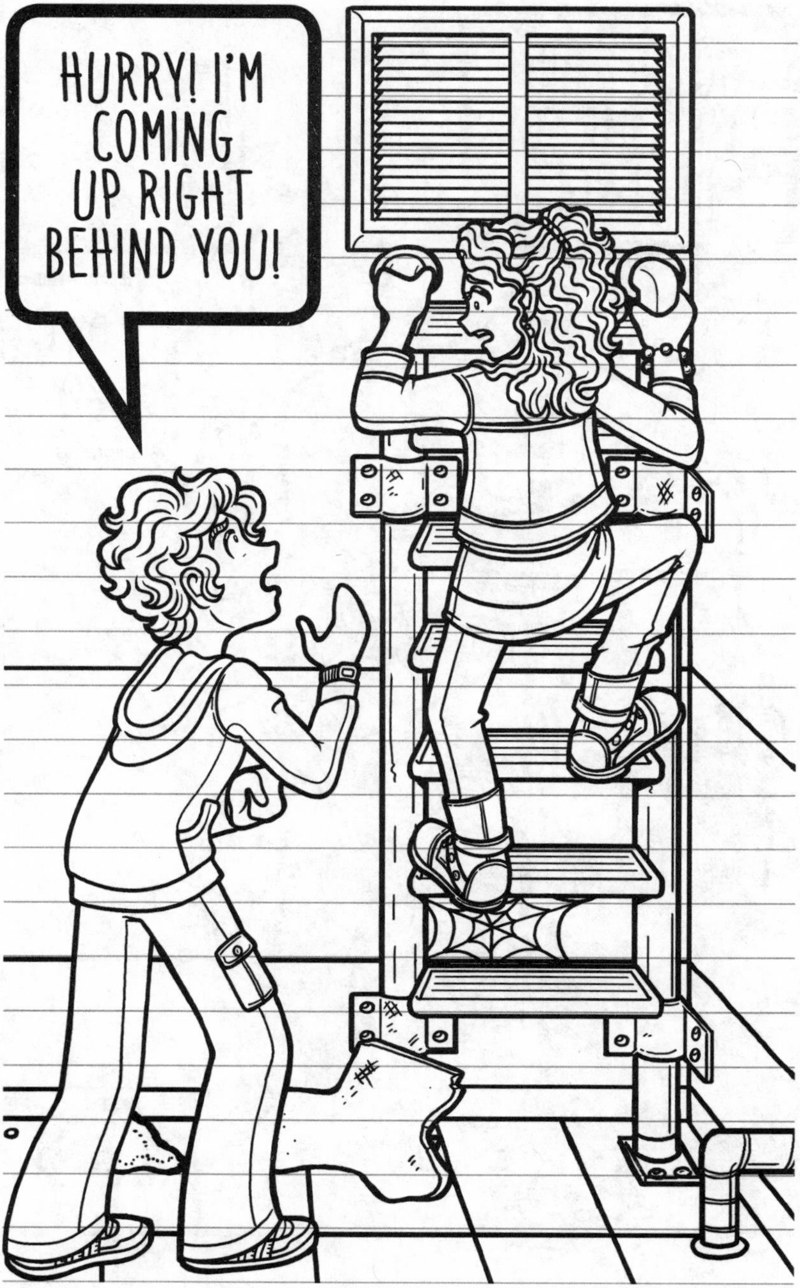
HURRY! I'M COMING UP RIGHT BEHIND YOU!

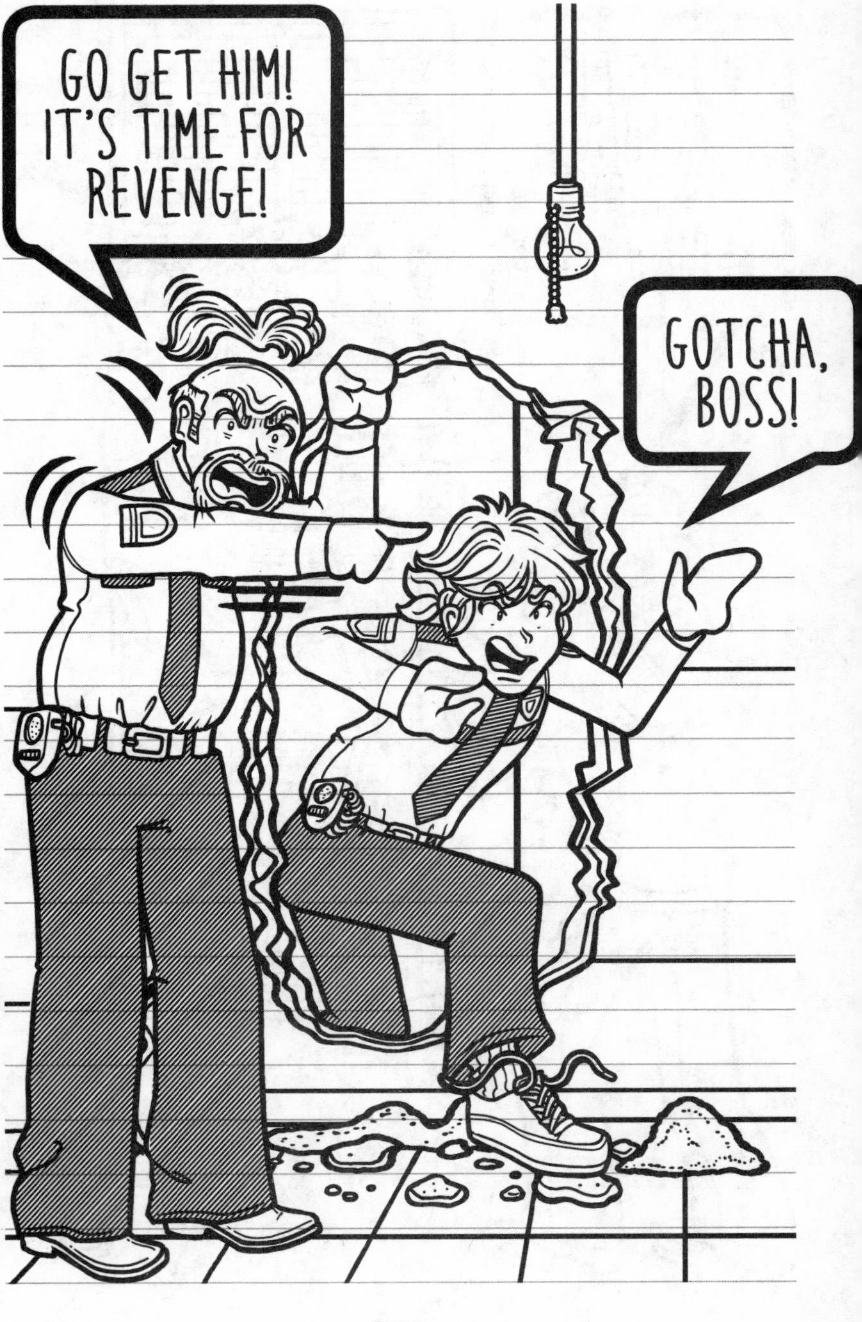
GO GET HIM! IT'S TIME FOR REVENGE!
GOTCHA, BOSS!

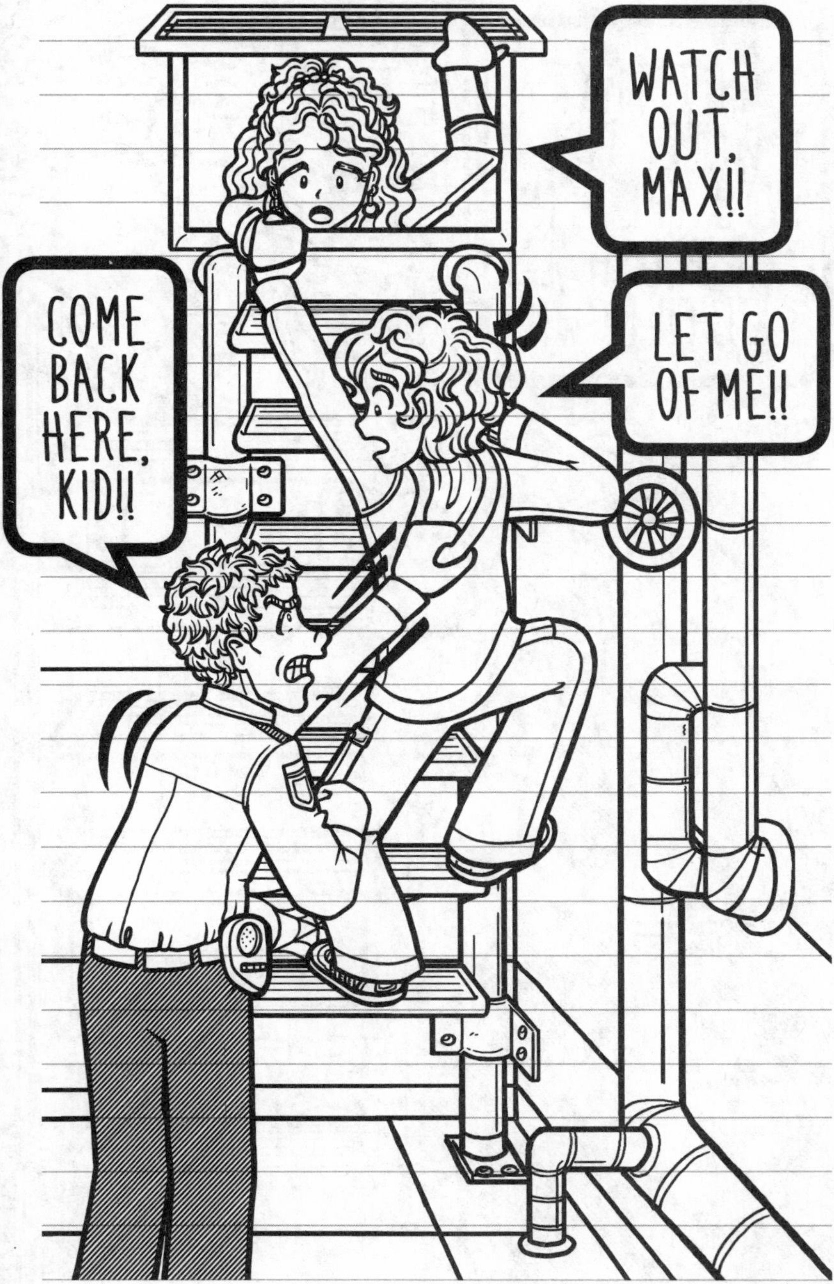
WATCH OUT, MAX!!
COME BACK HERE, KID!!
LET GO OF ME!!

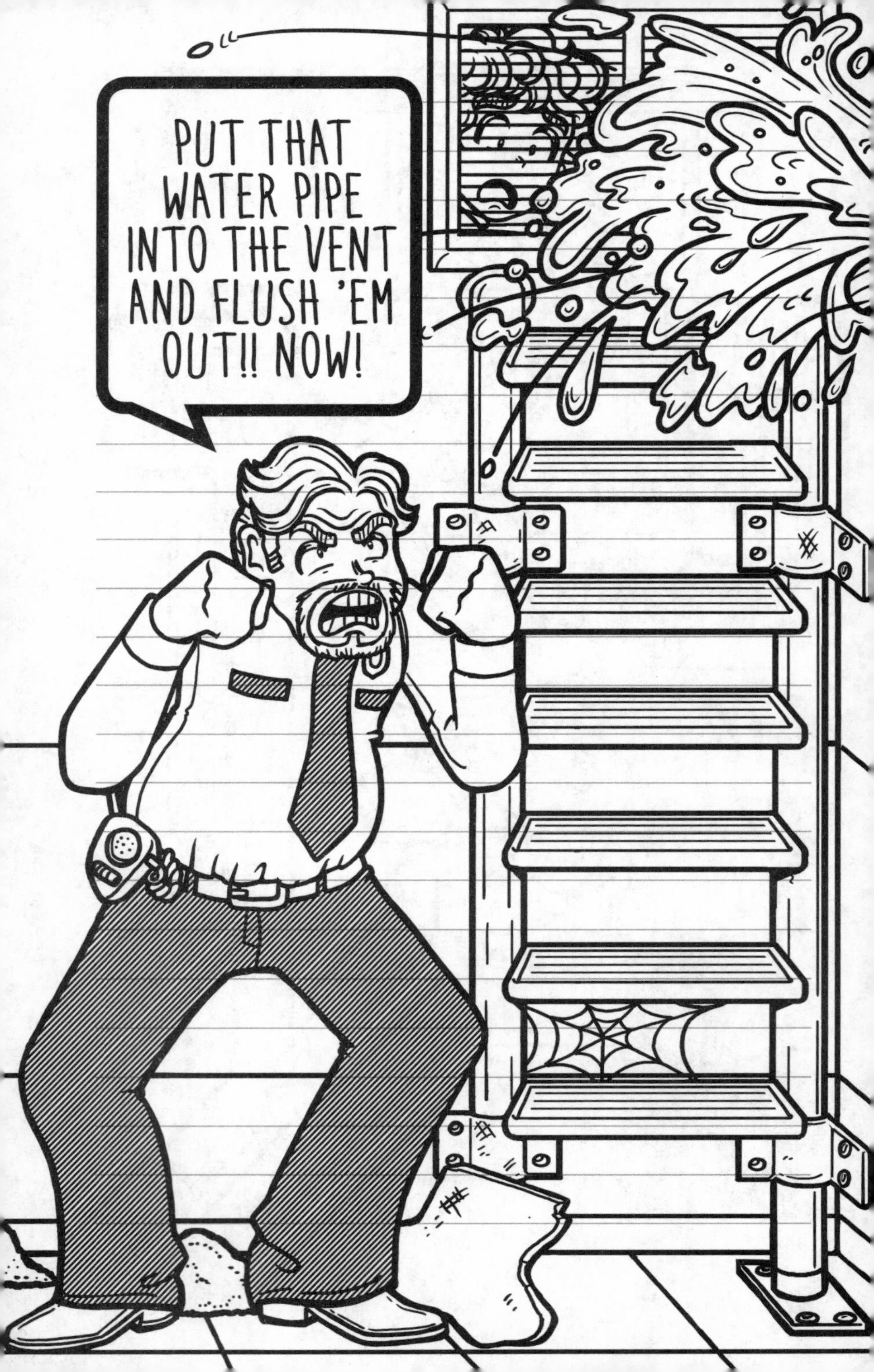
PUT THAT WATER PIPE INTO THE VENT AND FLUSH 'EM OUT!! NOW!

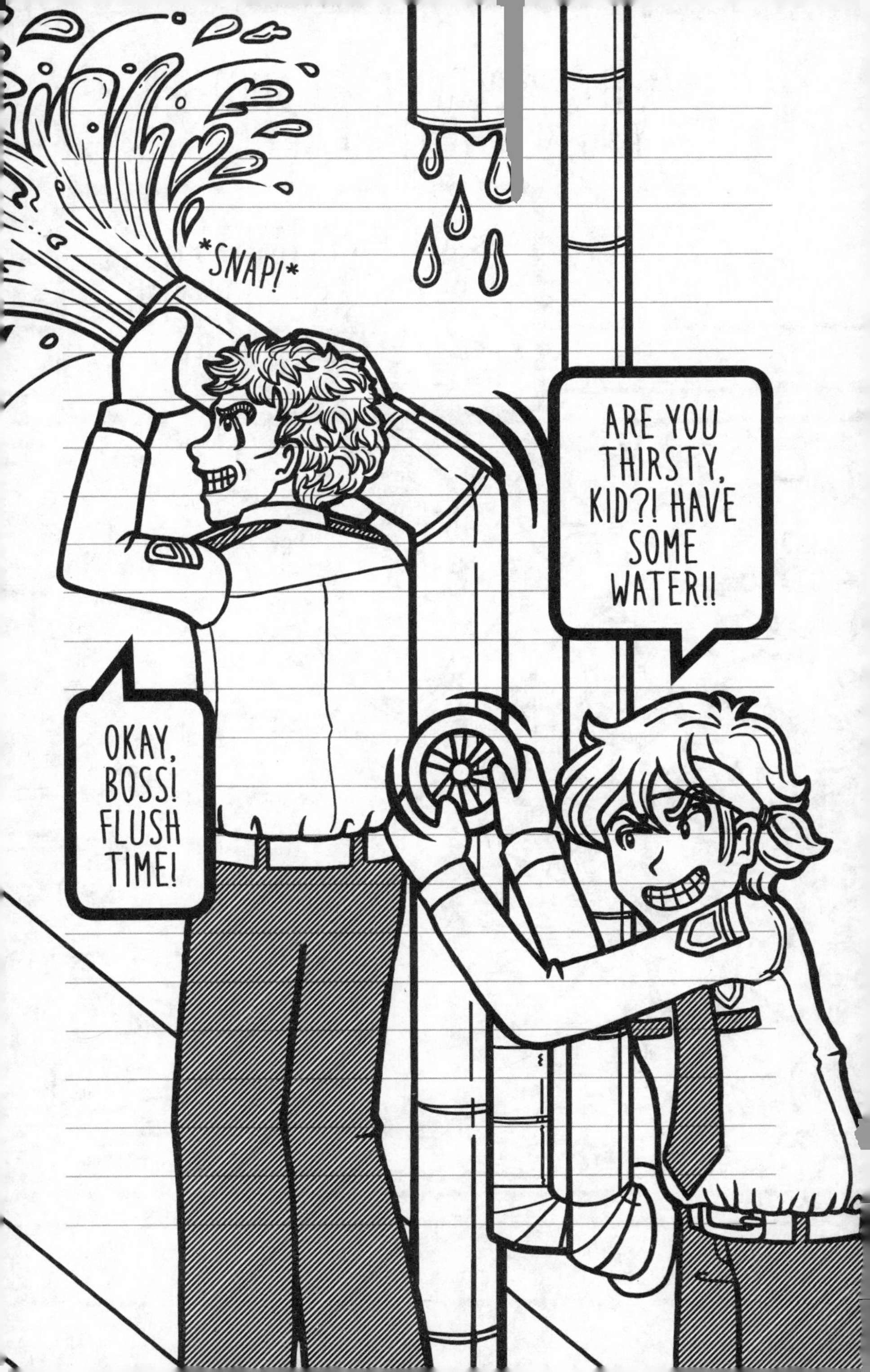
SNAP!
ARE YOU THIRSTY, KID?! HAVE SOME WATER!!
OKAY, BOSS! FLUSH TIME!

24. FLUSHED! EVEN YET ANOTHER MORTIFYING MISADVENTURE OF MAX CRUMBLY

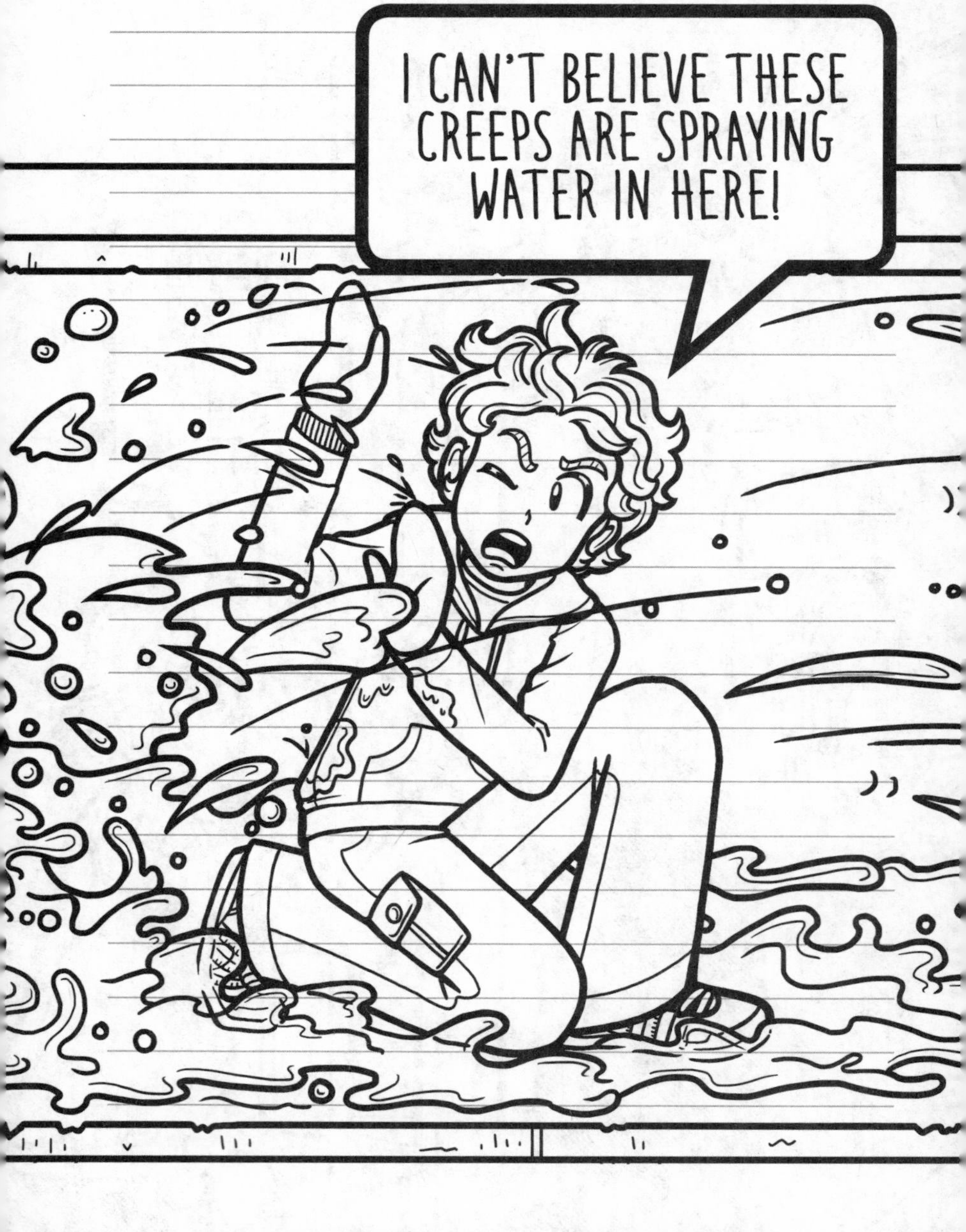
I CAN'T BELIEVE THESE CREEPS ARE SPRAYING WATER IN HERE!

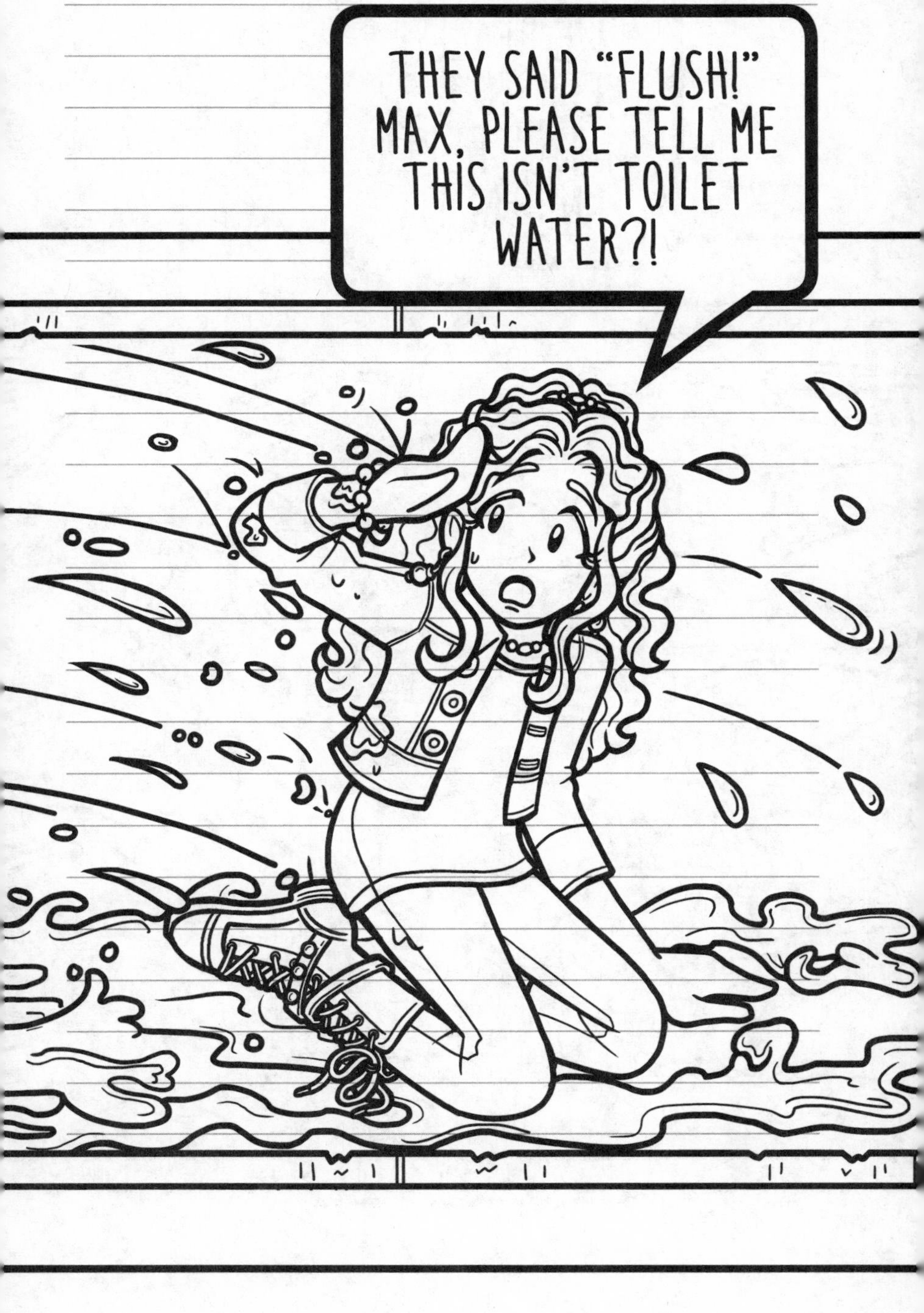
THEY SAID "FLUSH!" MAX, PLEASE TELL ME THIS ISN'T TOILET WATER?!

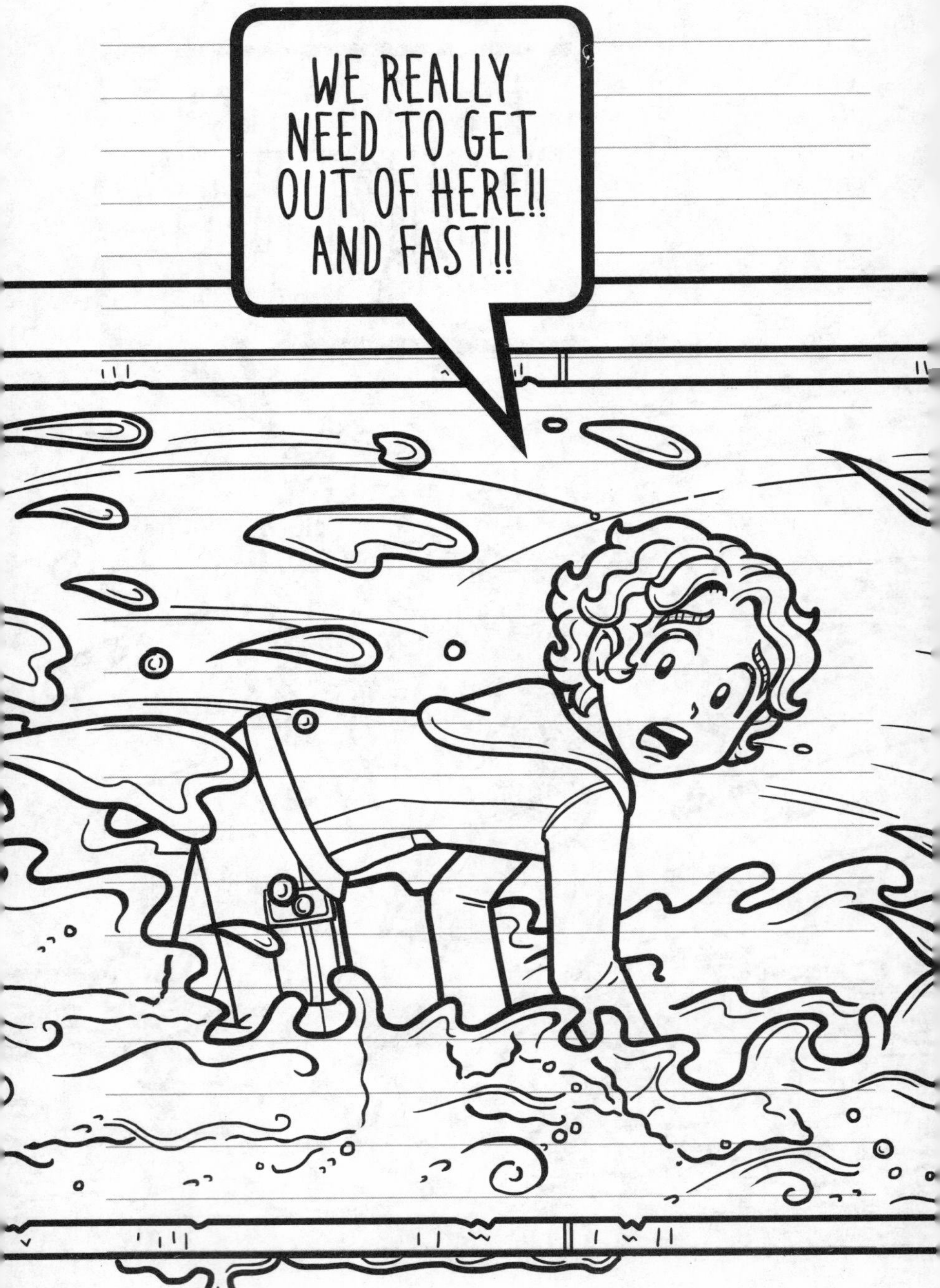
WE REALLY NEED TO GET OUT OF HERE!! AND FAST!!

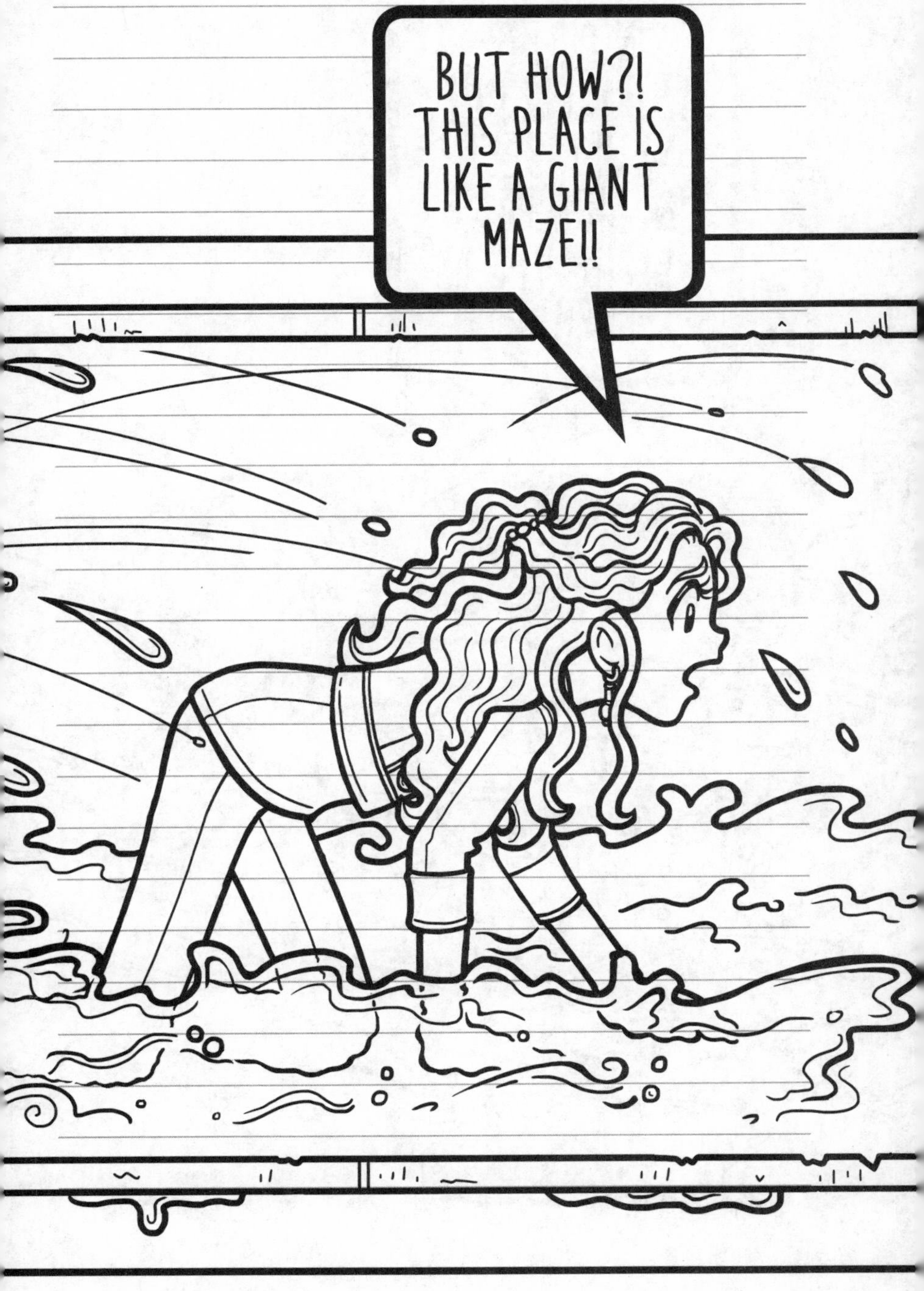
BUT HOW?! THIS PLACE IS LIKE A GIANT MAZE!!

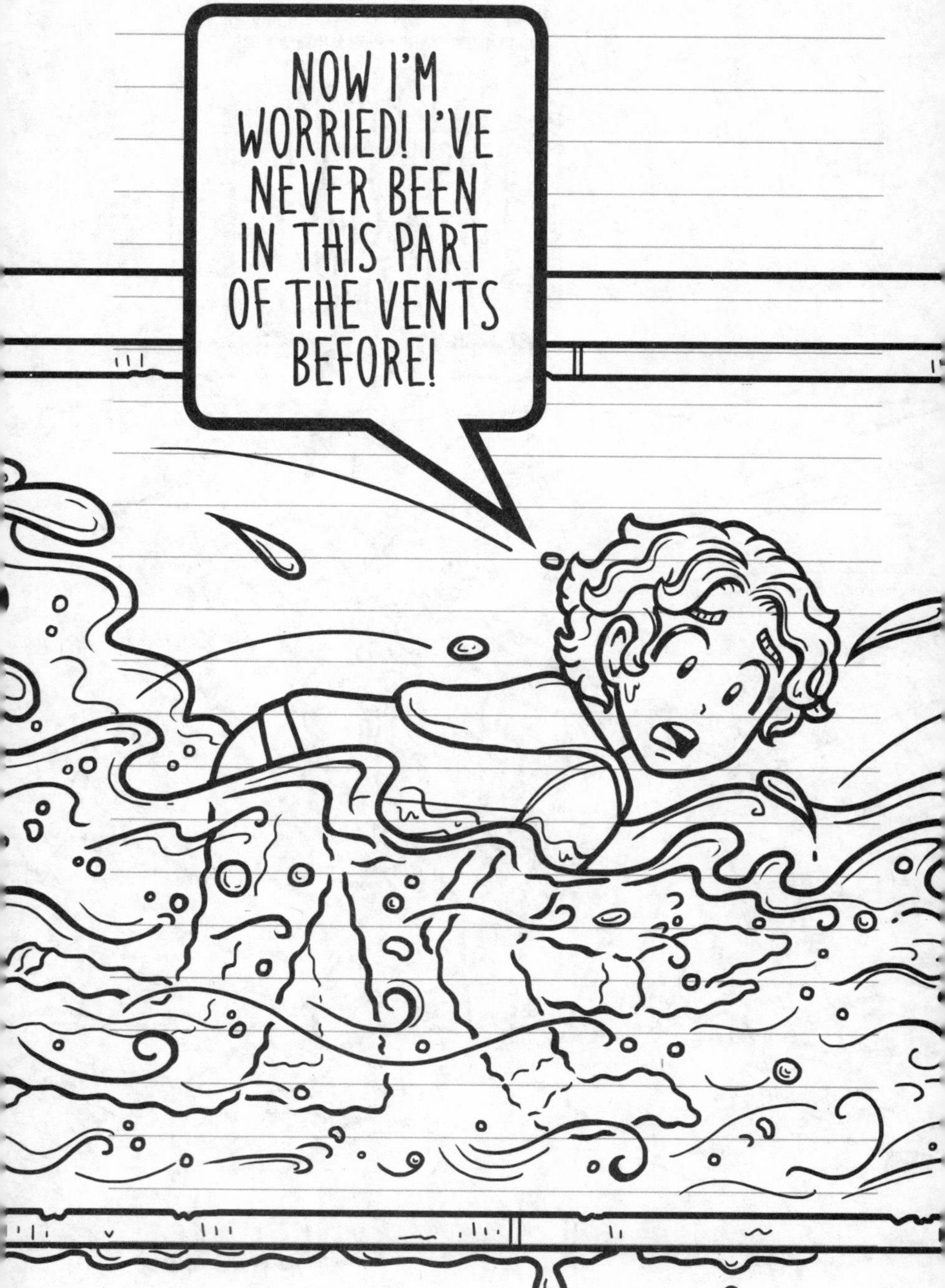
NOW I'M WORRIED! I'VE NEVER BEEN IN THIS PART OF THE VENTS BEFORE!

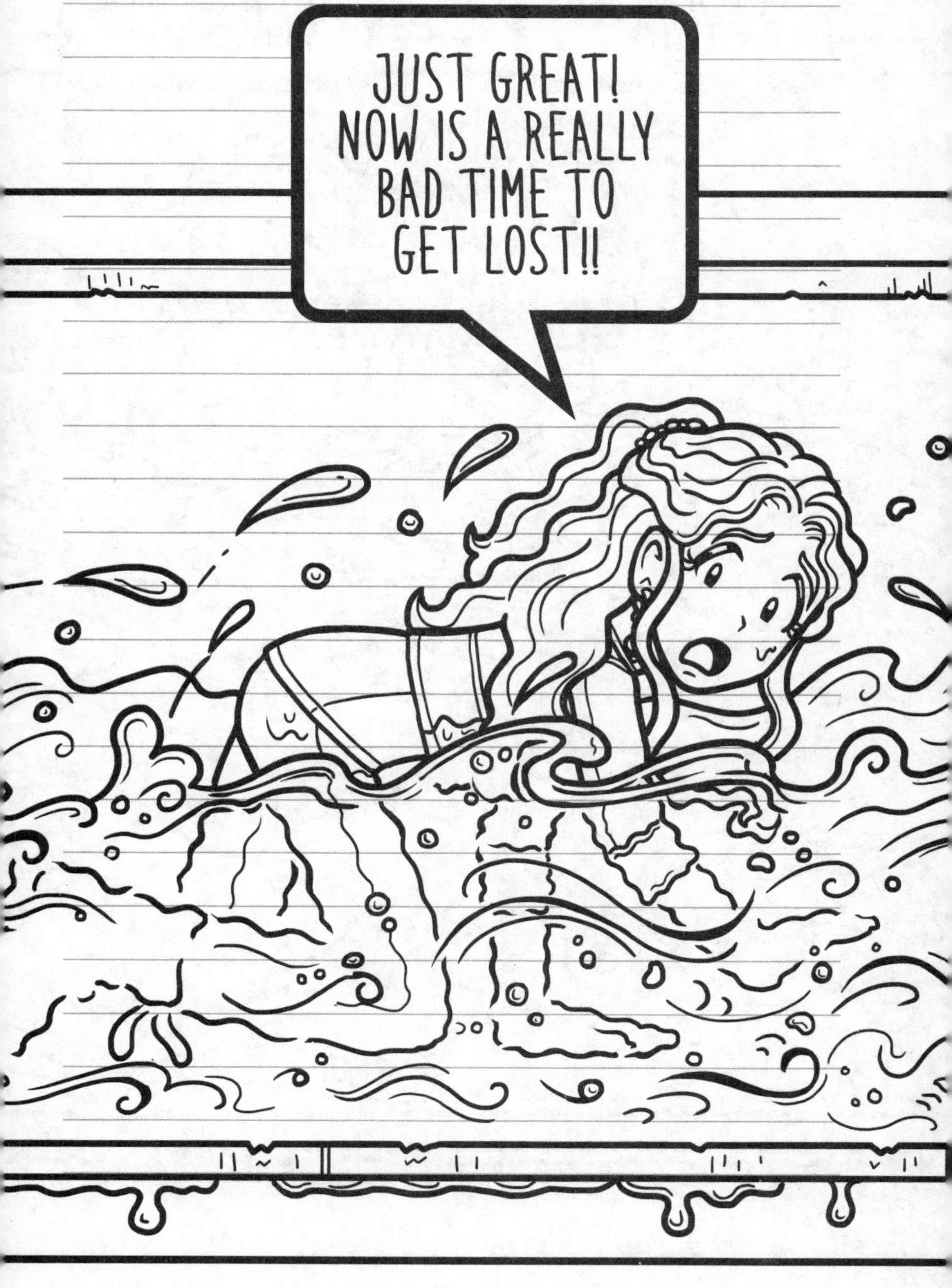
JUST GREAT! NOW IS A REALLY BAD TIME TO GET LOST!!

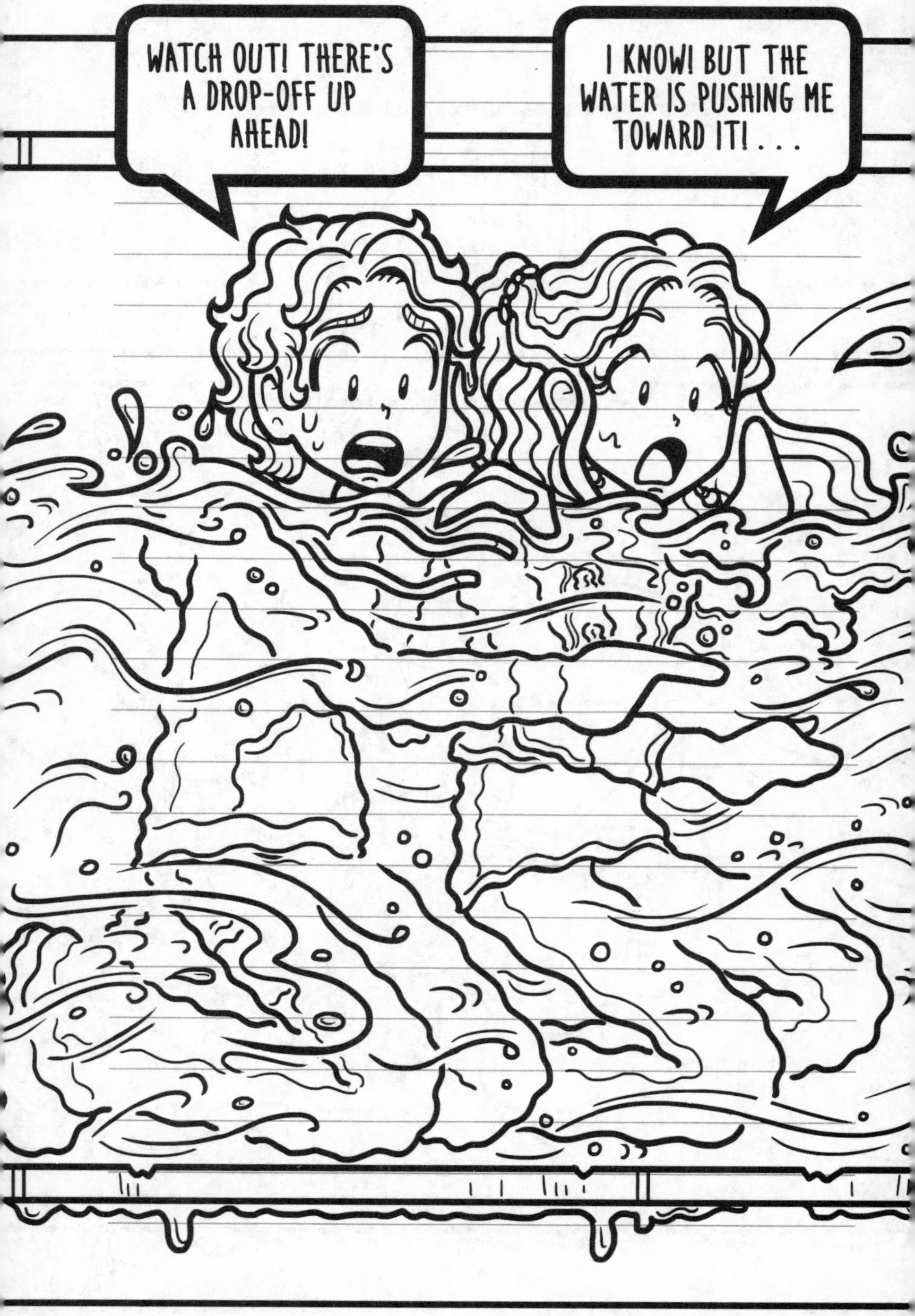
WATCH OUT! THERE'S A DROP-OFF UP AHEAD!
I KNOW! BUT THE WATER IS PUSHING ME TOWARD IT! . . .

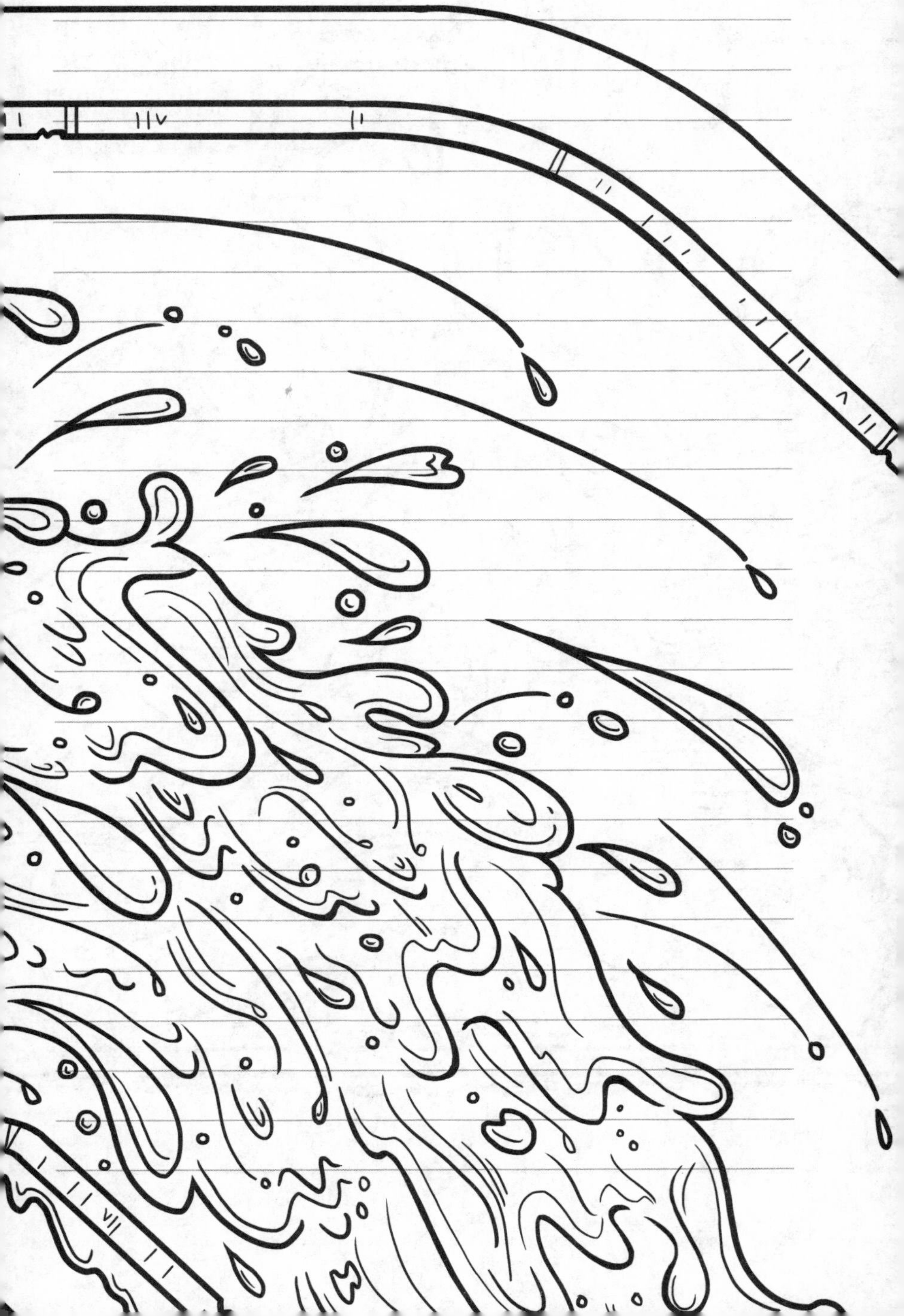

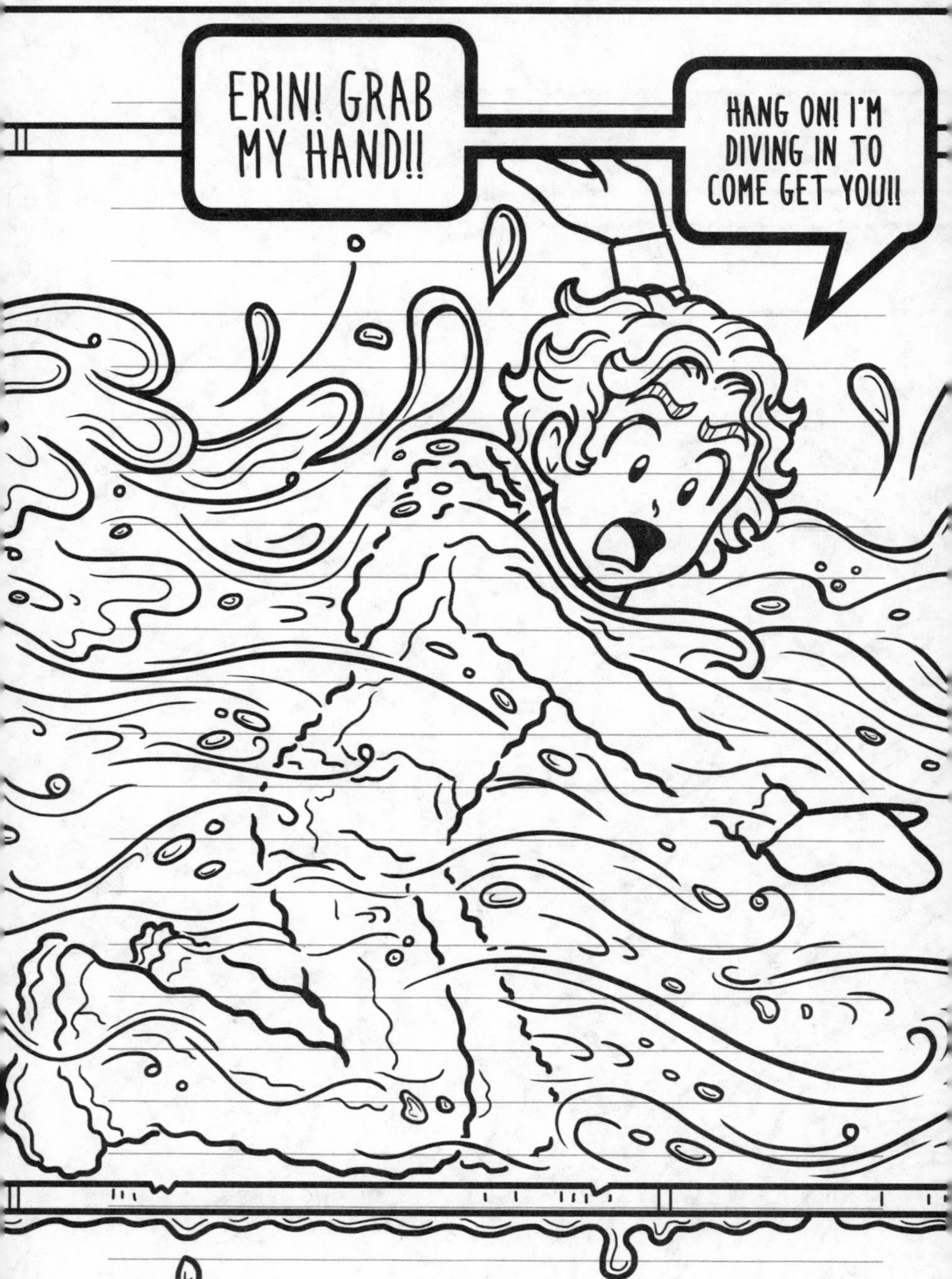
ERIN! GRAB MY HAND!!
HANG ON! I'M DIVING IN TO COME GET YOU!!

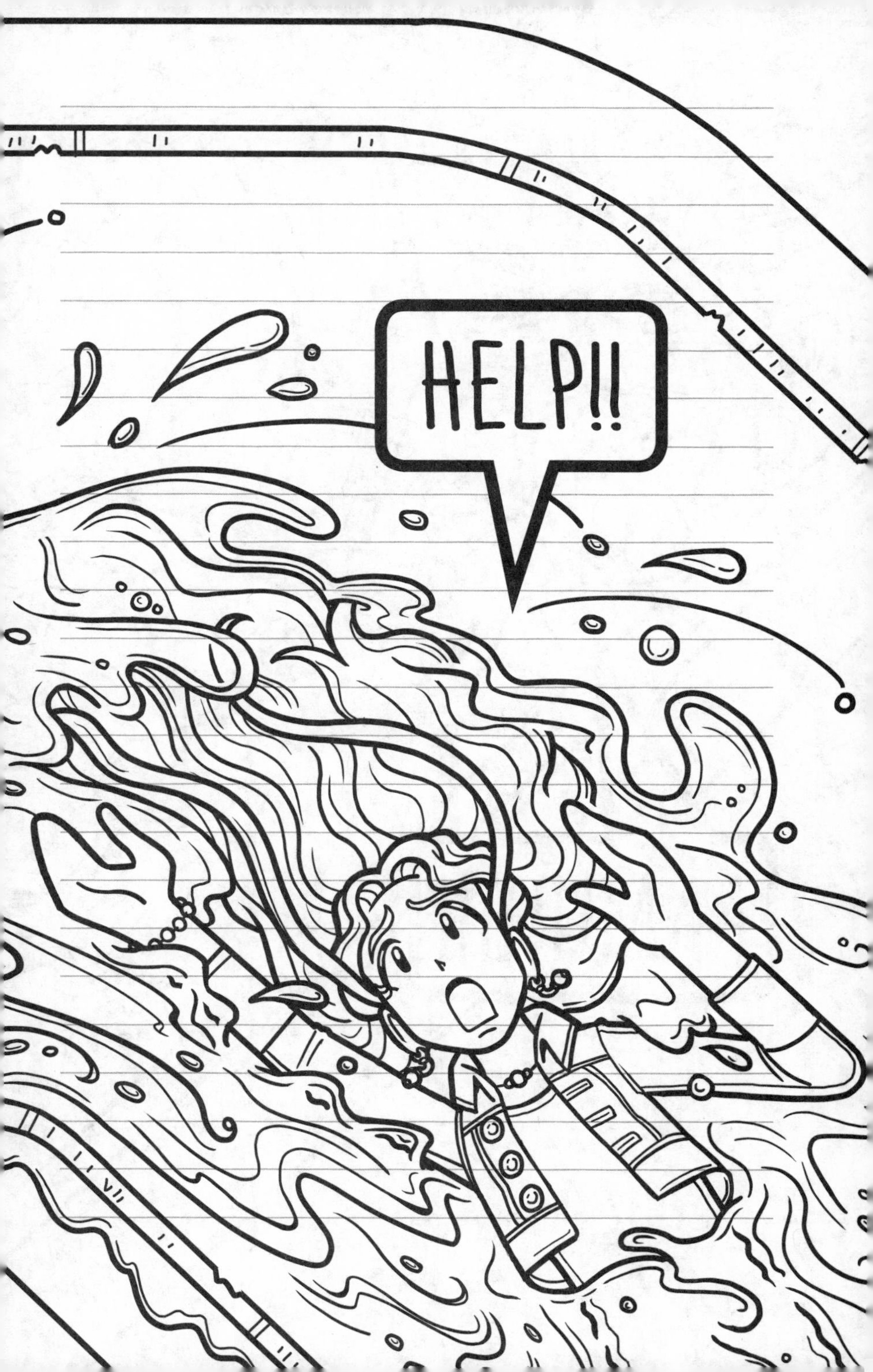
HELP!!

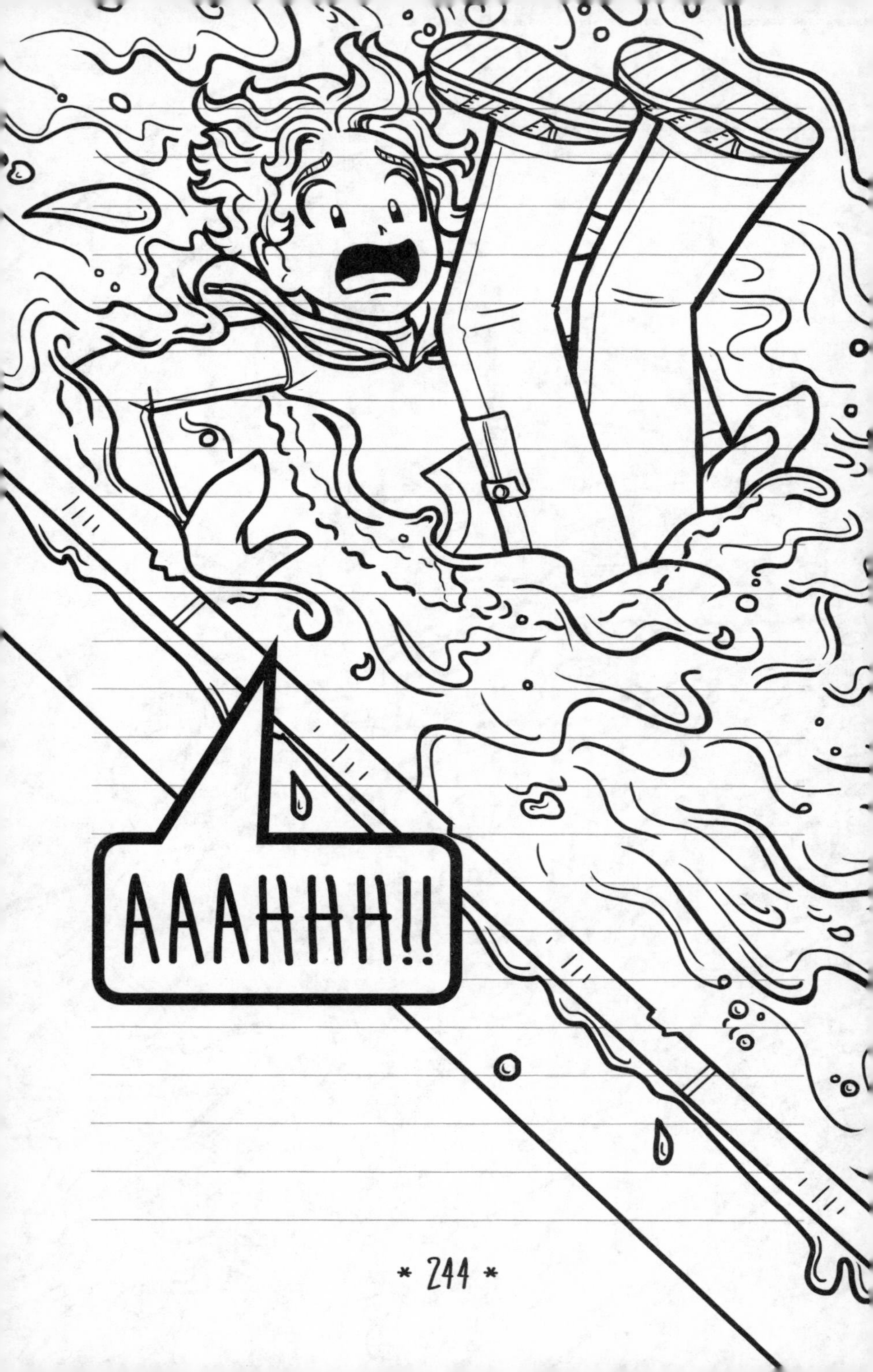
AAAHHH!!

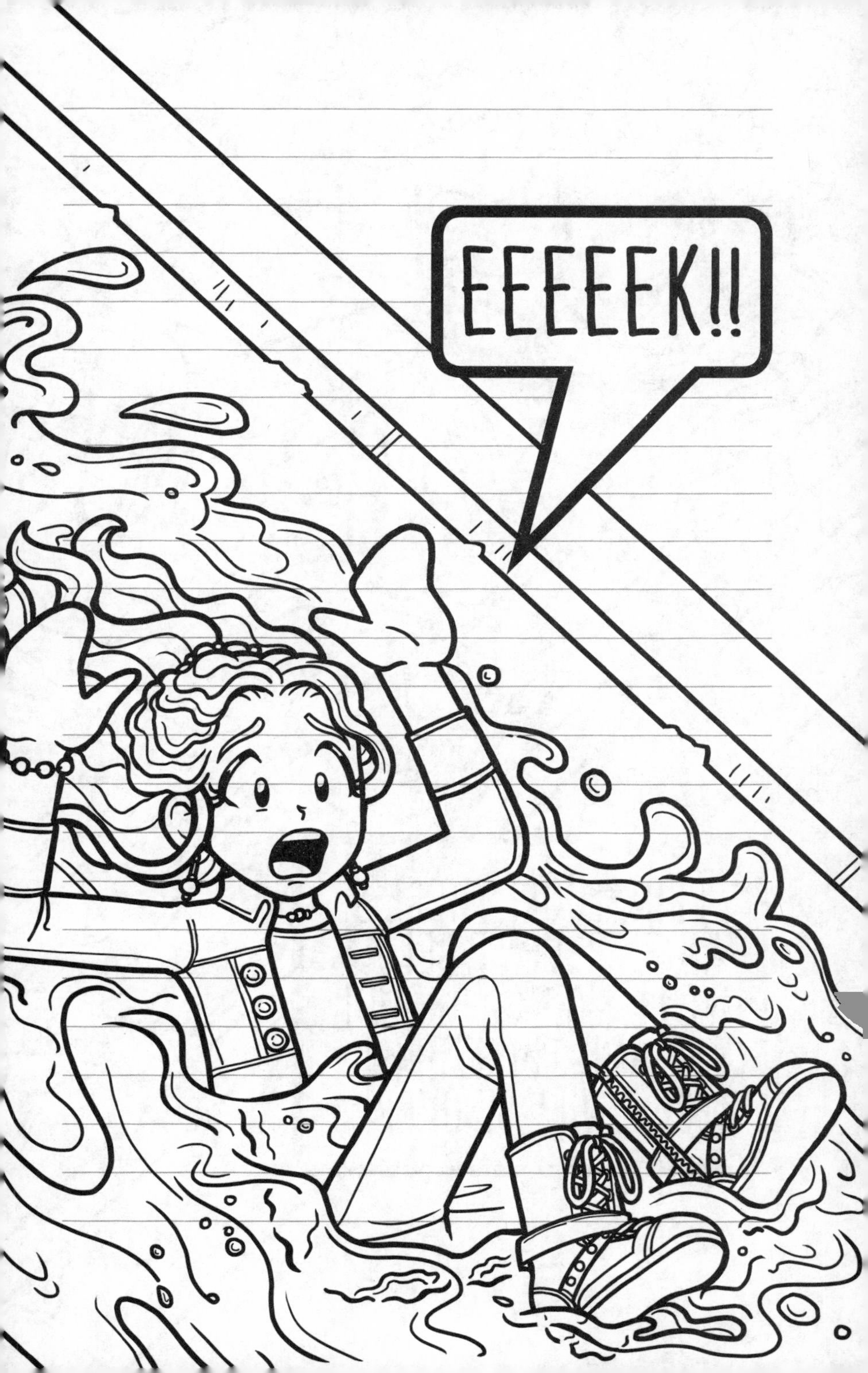
EEEEEK!!

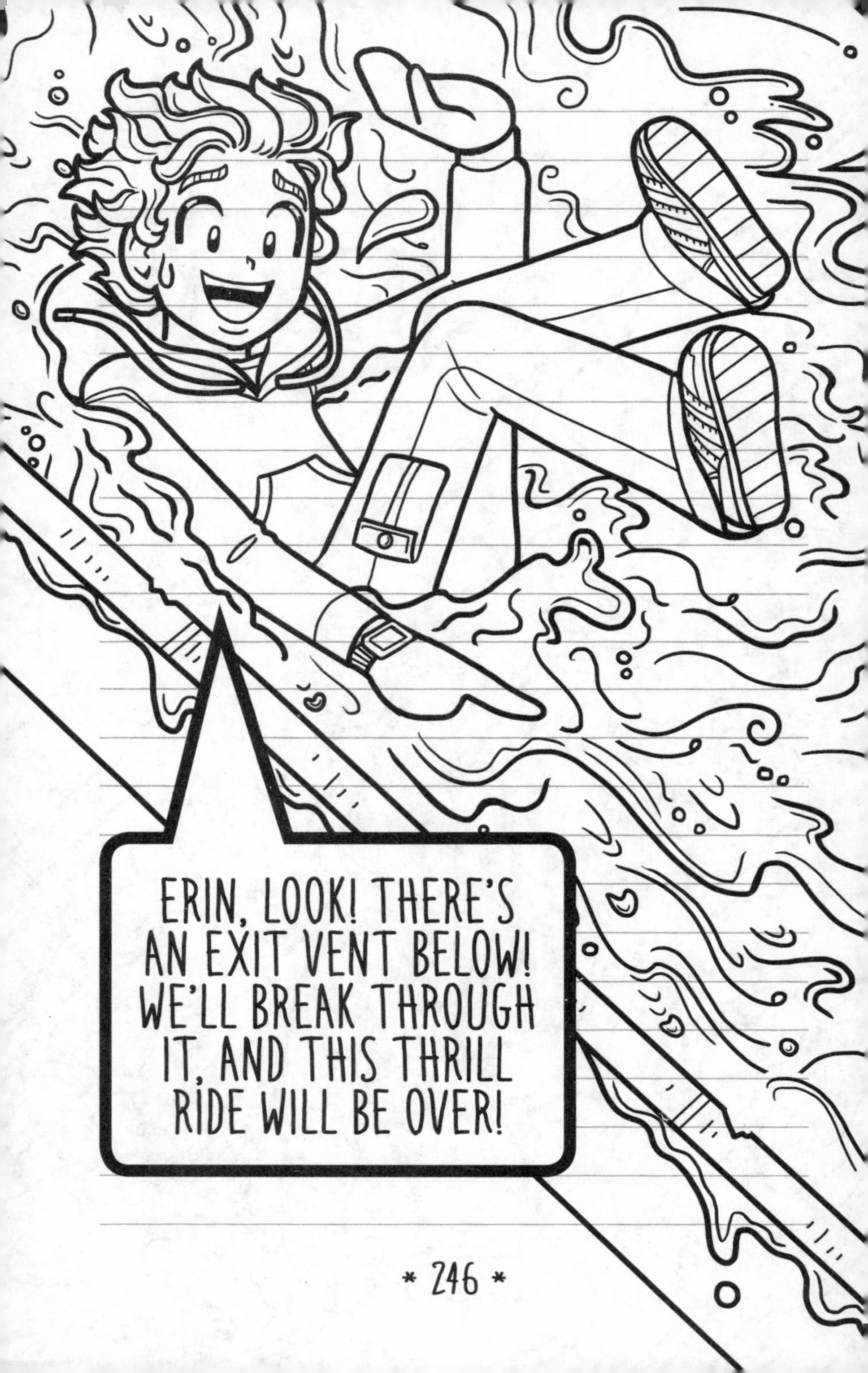
ERIN, LOOK! THERE'S AN EXIT VENT BELOW! WE'LL BREAK THROUGH IT, AND THIS THRILL RIDE WILL BE OVER!

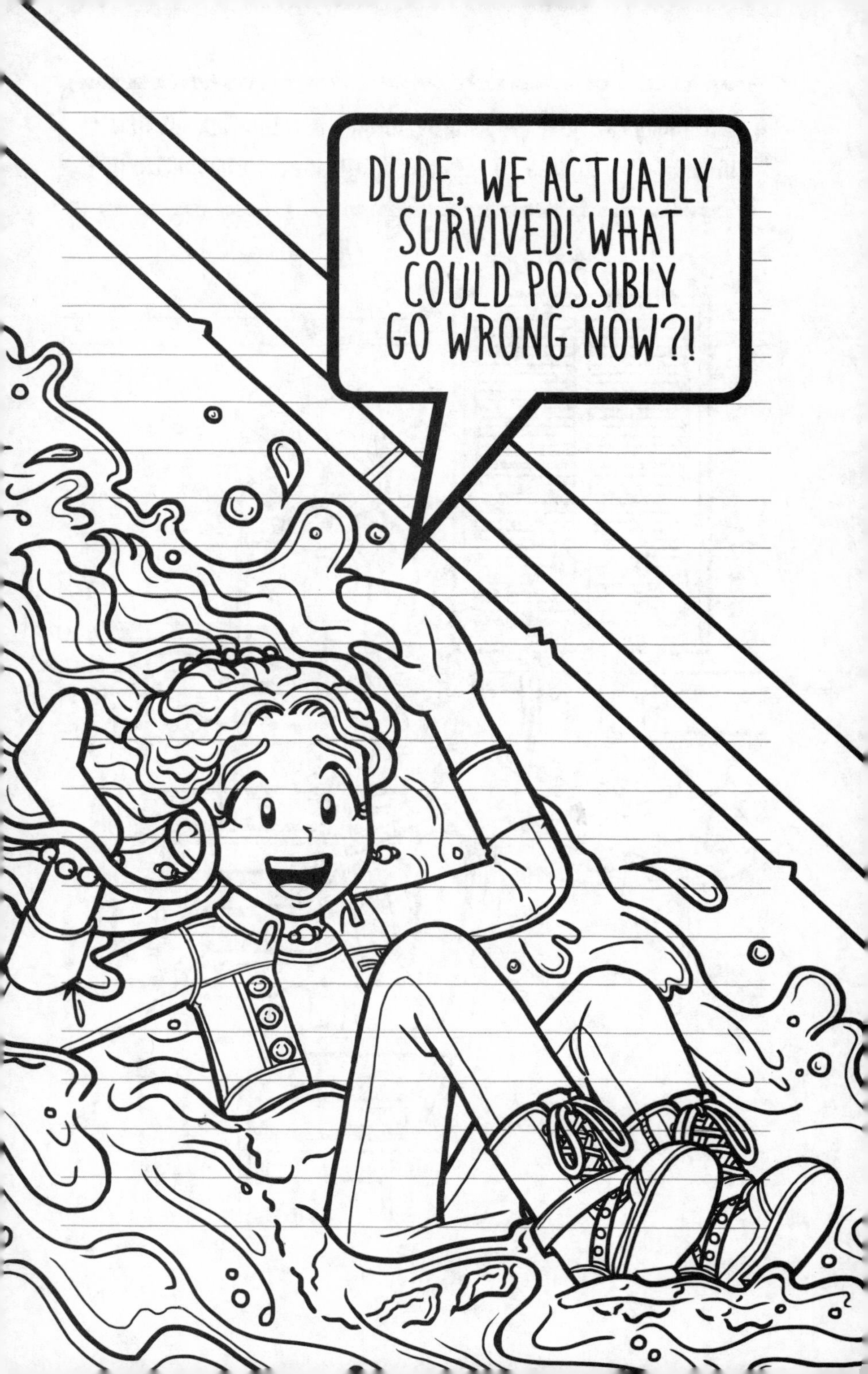
DUDE, WE ACTUALLY SURVIVED! WHAT COULD POSSIBLY GO WRONG NOW?!

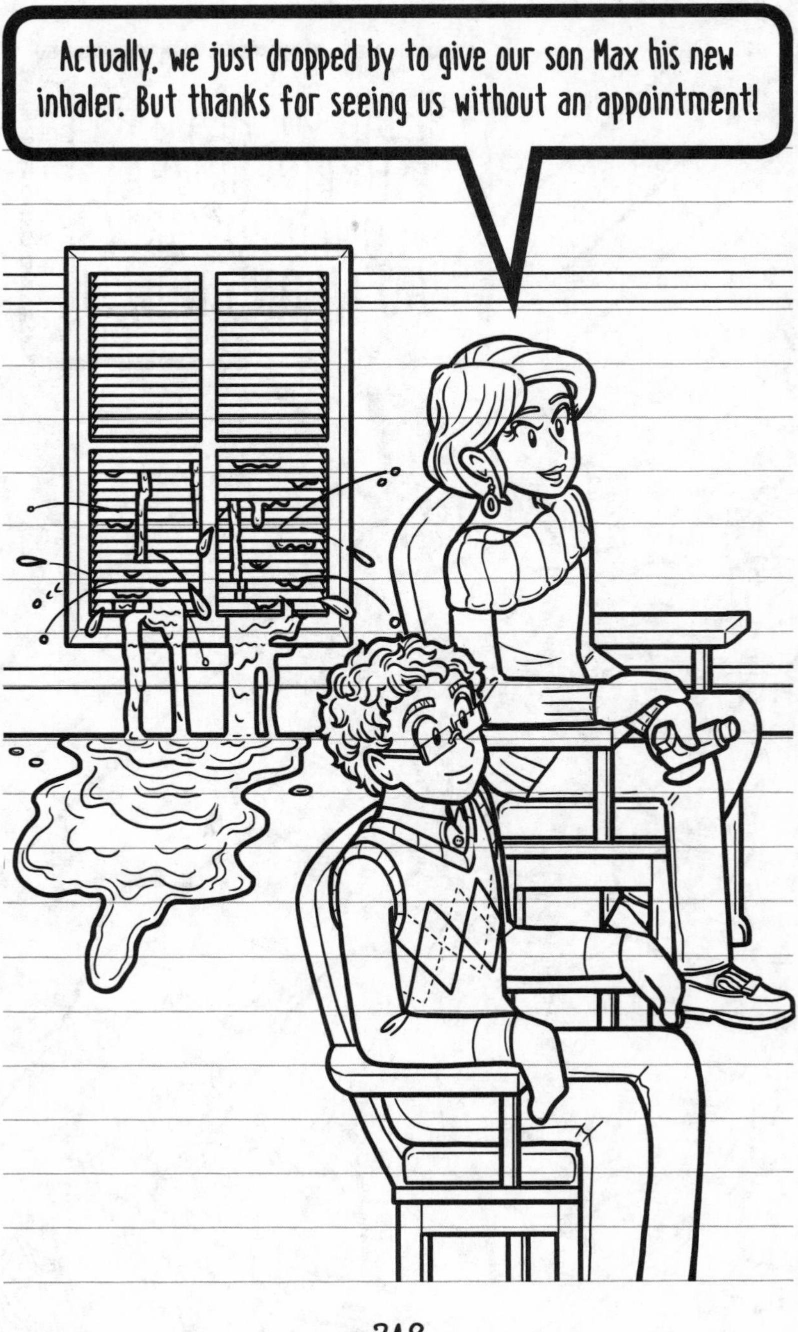
Actually, we just dropped by to give our son Max his new inhaler. But thanks for seeing us without an appointment!

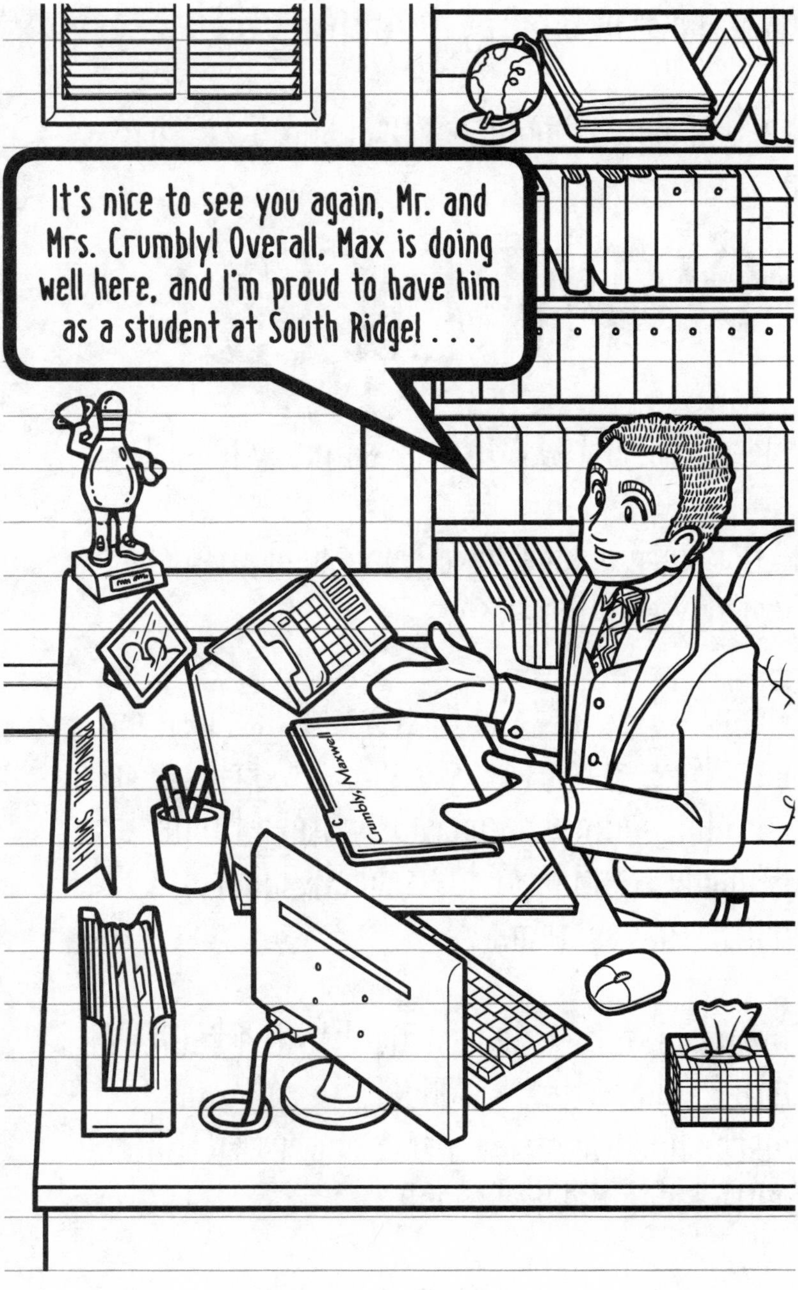
It's nice to see you again, Mr. and Mrs. Crumbly! Overall, Max is doing well here, and I'm proud to have him as a student at South Ridge! . . .
PRINCIPAL SMITH
C
Crumbly, Maxwell

Okay, now I'm totally FREAKING OUT!

The people sitting in Principal Smith's office are...

MY PARENTS!!

And that's just WRONG on so many levels!

If this were a superhero comic book, it would probably end like this:

When we last left the Masters of Mischief, our hero, Max, and his trusty sidekick, Erin, were barreling down a dangerously steep tunnel in a flooded section of the school's labyrinth-like ventilation system.

Unfortunately, it led straight to the PRINCIPAL'S OFFICE, where MAX'S PARENTS were in an unscheduled meeting discussing his FUTURE at South Ridge Middle School!

Will our courageous heroes dramatically CRASH into the room at ninety miles per hour in a massive man-made TIDAL WAVE ~~and rudely interrupt the meeting~~? Or will they somehow miraculously AVOID landing IN HOT WATER?

Will Max and Erin become suspects in the school break-in and remain sworn to secrecy?! Or will they SPILL their guts and end up shipwrecked in STORMY WATERS?

Will those fake security guards be successful in their second attempt at stealing the school's new computers? Or will their evil plot be BLOWN OUT OF THE WATER once again by our valiant heroes?

Will Thug get away with stealing that collectible comic book? Or will his devious plan go DOWN THE DRAIN when Max brilliantly outsmarts him?

And, finally, will Erin, the computer genius ~~and Max's crush~~, be cleared of false allegations

that SHE erased the school's security video?
Or will she be tossed headfirst into TROUBLED
WATERS?

Is this the FINAL misadventure of our soon-
to-be WASHED-UP heroes? Or will they somehow
triumph over adversity and resume their SECRET
lives fighting crime and protecting students
in the dank, dark halls of South Ridge Middle
School?

YES! I'm leaving you hanging **AGAIN!**

But I **WARNED YOU** about the CLIFFHANGER!

Right?!

If I can prevent what happened to ME from happening
to YOU or another kid, then every second Erin and
I spend almost drowning in those flooded vents will
be worth it.

And when you're DROWNING in doubt and FLOODED
with insecurities, just remember, if Erin and I

can become heroes and make the world a better place . . .

SO CAN YOU!

Just hang in there!

And KEEP YOUR HEAD ABOVE WATER!

YOU GOT THIS!

FOR REAL!

ACKNOWLEDGMENTS

Max is back as the Master of Mischief thanks to my incredibly talented and dedicated Superhero Squad.

To my editorial director, Liesa Abrams Mignogna (aka Batgirl), thank you for all that you do. Your ingenious master plan always saves the day.

Karin Paprocki, my brilliant art director, I'm always blown away by your incredible artistic feats. Katherine Devendorf, my managing editor, I'm highly impressed with your extraordinary editing prowess.

A special thanks to my superagent, Daniel Lazar. Your guidance, advice, and support are the secret source of my superpowers.

To my league of superheroes at Aladdin/Simon & Schuster: Mara Anastas, Chriscynethia Floyd, Jon Anderson, Julie Doebler, Caitlin Sweeny, Anna Jarzab, Alissa Nigro, Lauren Hoffman, Nicole Russo, Lauren Carr, Jenn Rothkin, Ian Reilly,

Christina Solazzo, Chelsea Morgan, Lauren Forte, Crystal Velasquez, Rebecca Vitkus, Michelle Leo, Sarah Woodruff, Christina Pecorale, Gary Urda, and the entire sales force. Thank you for your hard work and dedication, blasting through the galaxy to get these books into the hands of children around the world.

Torie Doherty-Munro at Writers House, and my Writers House foreign rights agents, Cecilia de la Campa and James Munro, thank you for your energetic intergalactic support.

A special thanks to Deena, Zoé, Marie, and Joy for your powerful force field of creativity and teamwork.

To my super-talented and awesome sidekick (and daughter) Nikki—your masterful and brilliant illustrations bring Max's fascinating world to life.

My manager, Kim; my assistant, Arianna; and my entire family, thank you for your heroic support and unwavering love.

RACHEL RENÉE RUSSELL

is the #1 *New York Times* bestselling author of the blockbuster book series Dork Diaries and the exciting series The Misadventures of Max Crumbly.

There are more than forty-five million copies of her books in print worldwide, and they have been translated into thirty-six languages.

She enjoys working with her daughter Nikki, who helps illustrate her books.

Rachel's message is "Become the hero you've always admired!"

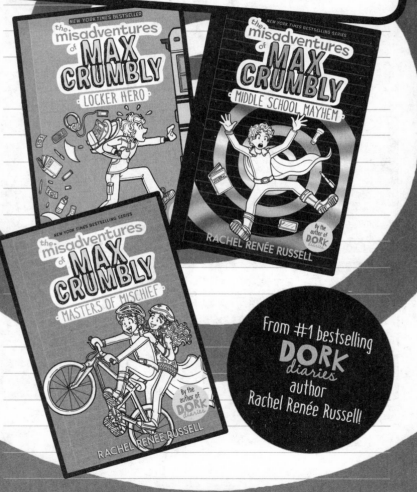

Max is about to face the scariest place he's ever been—South Ridge Middle School!

Have YOU read all of

by Rachel Renée Russell

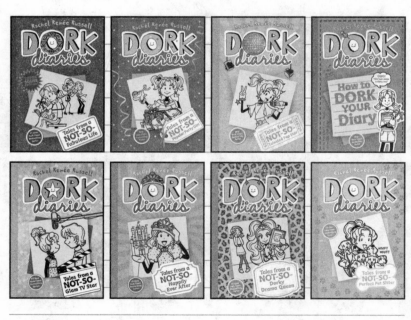

Nikki Maxwell's diaries?

MOST IMPORTANT TIP EVER FROM NIKKI MAXWELL:

Always let your inner **DORK** shine through!

#1 New York Times Bestselling Series